THE REVENGE GAME
WICKLOW COLLEGE OF THE ARCANE ARTS
BOOK II

BR KINGSOLVER

By BR Kingsolver

brkingsolver.com

Cover art by Heather Hamilton-Senter
www.bookcoverartistry.com

Copyright 2023 BR Kingsolver

❦ Created with Vellum

LICENSE NOTES

This book is licensed for your personal enjoyment only. All rights reserved. No part of this book may be reproduced or transmitted in any form or by any means now known or hereinafter invented, electronic or mechanical, including but not limited to photocopying, recording, or by an information storage and retrieval system, without the written permission of the Publisher, except where permitted by law.

In ebook or other electronic format, it may not be re-sold or given away to other people. If you would like to share this book with another person, please purchase an additional copy for each recipient. If you're reading this book and did not purchase it, or it was not purchased for your use only, then please return it and purchase your own copy. Thank you for respecting the hard work of this author.

Get updates on new book releases, promotions, contests and giveaways! Sign up for my newsletter.

Wicklow College of Arcane Arts
The Gambler Grimoire
The Revenge Game

The Rift Chronicles
Magitek**
War Song**
Soul Harvest**

The Crossroad Chronicles
Family Ties
Night Market
Ruby Road

Rosie O'Grady's Paranormal Bar and Grill
Shadow Hunter**
Night Stalker**
Dark Dancer**
Well of Magic**
Knights Magica**

The Dark Streets Series
Gods and Demons**
Dragon's Egg**
Witches' Brew**

The Chameleon Assassin Series
Chameleon Assassin**
Chameleon Uncovered**
Chameleon's Challenge**
Chameleon's Death Dance**
Diamonds and Blood**

The Telepathic Clans Saga
The Succubus Gift
Succubus Unleashed
Broken Dolls
Succubus Rising
Succubus Ascendant

Other books
I'll Sing for my Dinner
Trust

CHAPTER 1

Alice Henderson was a legend at Wicklow College long before she took a header three and a half stories from her apartment window to the sidewalk below.

We were sharing a bottle of wine, sitting on my front stoop across the breezeway from the stairway door leading to Alice's apartment. Watching the forensics people and police go in and out was the most exciting thing happening at the college on a Friday afternoon.

We weren't in position to see the body or any of the activity around that. Her remains were on the other side of the building, and the police had all that cordoned off.

"There were rumors—which she did nothing to discourage—that she worked for the CIA back in the fifties and sixties," Kelly Grace, the college librarian and archivist, told me. "I had her as a professor—the last time twelve years ago—before they finally stopped assigning her classes. She was getting a little absent-minded. At one point, she gave the same lecture three classes in a row—verbatim, someone recorded them. Sometimes she'd wander off topic and tell us about her love affairs.

One of them sounded an awful lot like the script for *Casablanca*."

"I find it amazing they've allowed her to keep that apartment after she was no longer an employee," I said.

"Where would she go?" Kelly asked. "She didn't have any close family, and she lived in that apartment the past thirty years. She probably felt she was being generous by not charging the college rent."

I chuckled. "I do hope I'm not still here in thirty years. There has to be a life after Wicklow."

David Hamilton, who lived directly across the breezeway from me and downstairs from Alice, wandered over and leaned against the wall.

"The police at first thought it might be a suicide," he said, "until I pointed out that Alice was eighty-five, used a cane, and probably wasn't able to climb up on the table in front of that window. She couldn't even climb the stairs to her apartment. The college installed a stair lift for her several years ago."

"I heard someone say something about a note?" I asked.

David nodded. "Sam Kagan showed me an enigmatic note—not in Alice's handwriting—that didn't sound at all like a suicide note. Actually sounded a little threatening."

I perked up my ears. "Ooo. What did it say?"

David and Kelly laughed.

"Are you going to play Miss Marple?" Kelly asked.

"Got any better ideas? Wicklow is definitely lacking in what I consider normal forms of entertainment."

"You have no proof," David said.

"Huh?" Kelly and I said in unison.

"That's what the note said."

"How do you know it wasn't her handwriting?" I asked.

He gave me an indulgent smile. "She leaves me notes. Alice hasn't driven in twenty years, so she has me stop by the liquor store for her. She gets her groceries delivered, but the liquor store won't do that. Or, at least they didn't in the past. I haven't bothered to check if they do now."

"What kind of liquor?" Kelly asked. "Sherry?"

He shook his head. "Aged single malt scotch. Sometimes she remembers to reimburse me for it."

"Well," Kelly said, "I hope the cops clear this up soon. This may sound terrible, but I can't wait to get my hands on her private papers."

"I guess archivists have their priorities," I said, looking at David and rolling my eyes.

"It's the book," Kelly replied. "I'm writing her biography, and she held back a bunch of her private papers until after she died. If I can get them, I can finish the book and publish it. I get half the royalties, and the other half goes to her estate."

"Assuming that wasn't why she was killed, and the papers haven't been stolen," I said.

Kelly shook her head. "No, most of them are in the archives in the library. She may have more in her rooms, though. I must say that this isn't the ending I expected."

David shook his head. "I doubt anyone waited until she was eighty-five to kill her over some old papers. Hell, she has to have outlived all of her enemies."

"Maybe she levitated out the window," I said.

Kelly shrugged "If she could levitate, she wouldn't have needed the stair lift."

"Would you like some wine?" I asked David as I stood to go refill my glass. "Kelly? A refill?"

When both of them said yes, I simply brought the bottle out with a fresh glass for David. A few minutes later, Lieutenant Sam Kagan of the Wicklow City Police strolled over to us.

"I've already spoken with Dr. Hamilton. Did either of you see or hear anything?"

Kelly and I shook our heads.

"You folks were already here when I came by after I got off work," Kelly said.

"The first I knew anything had happened was when I heard the sirens," I told him. "I was out in the greenhouse. Any signs of a struggle? Or maybe someone searched the place for hidden treasure once they tossed her out?"

He gave me an exasperated look. "We don't know what happened. The window is open, and she fell out."

"Yeah," I said, "pretty clumsy of her. You'd think she'd know where that window was after living there for thirty years."

"I don't need you doing any amateur sleuthing."

"Of course not. I barely knew the woman." I had actually had dinner with her once at the Faculty Club. She invited me, asked a lot of nosey questions, and stuck me with the bill. Otherwise, the extent of our relationship was to exchange greetings on the occasional times we passed each other while walking about the campus.

I had promised Kelly that I would proofread the chapters as she finished them. I also offered to format the manuscript. I had published two books of my own and remembered the picky little things my editors had whined about.

Kagan started to turn away, but I called to him. "Lieutenant?"

"Yes, Dr. Robinson?"

"Please don't forget to clean out the refrigerator." I gave him my sweetest poisonous smile.

He glowered at me, and I batted my eyes at him. The police had barred entrance to the last murder scene at Wicklow for six months, and the refrigerator had turned into a toxic mess. In the end, they didn't clean the refrigerator, they just threw it away.

"What did she teach?" I asked as the wine ran out and I started thinking about dinner.

"She was an illusionist," David said. "She also had some

talent as an alchemist. Quite a strong witch. Both talents would have been rather handy when she was with the CIA."

"Is that real?" I asked. "I mean, did she really work for the CIA? Other than as a secretary?"

"I'll let you know as soon as I can get my hands on all her papers," Kelly said. "Supposedly, that's why she held them back. Top secret, you know? She said if the book came out before she died, the spooks in Washington would come looking for her."

"What did your father have to say about that?" I asked. Kelly's father was English and had spent most of his career stationed in the U.S. Based on a few things she had said, I suspected he was with MI-6.

Kelly shrugged. "He said his contacts in U.S. intelligence had heard of her, but he's twenty years younger than she was. I'm hungry. Anyone else?"

CHAPTER 2

"Savanna, someone else you know supposedly worked for an intelligence service," David said after we had ordered dinner at the Faculty Club.

"Oh, really? And who might that be?" I asked.

"Lowell Carragher." The way David eyed me, looking for a reaction, made me determined not to react at all. Lowell owned a local bookstore, and I had been to dinner with him a couple of times. Lowell and David were fishing buddies, and I suspected both might be fishing for a more intimate acquaintance than I had shared with either.

"CIA?" I asked.

"Naval Intelligence. He was in the Navy for ten years. Spent much of it in South America. Alice was teaching here at that time, so I doubt he could shed much light on her spying activities."

"I've heard the Bolivian Navy is a major national security threat," Kelly said, winking at me.

David shrugged. "I know he's fluent in Spanish. We took a trip down to Argentina together, and he knew the place quite well."

"Was Alice a linguist?" I asked.

"French, Spanish, German, Russian," Kelly answered. "Probably a smattering of other languages, but she has books in those languages on her shelves. Gave me a lecture once on the beauty of Dostoevsky's prose."

"She was a beauty in her day," David said.

Kelly nodded. "And from what she shared with me, she used her looks shamelessly in the service of her country."

"What about her time here? Did you say she was at Wicklow for thirty years?"

Kelly became quite animated. "She was a fascinating woman. Taught both magic and history. One of the last full professors who didn't hold a doctorate. Very involved with students, and served on the Faculty Council forever. Losing her seat there was her major disappointment when she retired."

"She was very close with Jerome Carver," David said. "It was rumored that they had an affair years ago. She was twenty years older than him, but that wouldn't have stopped her. She made a pass at me last week. She's been doing it for twenty years. It was sort of a game we played."

Carver was the Dean of Academics, and the man who hired me. I had heard from others that he was a philanderer, in spite of being married to a woman ten years his junior.

I grinned at him. "What do you think she'd have done if you accepted?"

He didn't even blush. "Stripped me down in a New York minute. Probably had me right there on the stairs. Alice was neither bashful nor coy." He winked at me. "When you live downstairs from someone for twenty-five years, you hear a lot of things. Alice wasn't a quiet lover."

"Did she have any health problems that you know of?" I asked.

They both shook their heads.

"Other than old age, no," David said. "She was getting a

little senile, but since she didn't get out much anymore, that really didn't cause any problems. I never saw her depressed."

After we ate dinner, I asked, "Would you consider me morbid for wanting to see where this happened? I've actually never walked around that side of the building before." I'd been at Wicklow for two months, and much of the college and the town remained unexplored.

"If the police don't still have it closed off," David said.

We left through the back door of the Faculty Club, which let out across from the library and museum. We walked past a parking lot used primarily by visitors and those attending concerts and theatrical performances at the president's mansion. The college had the largest theater and provided most of the cultural events in the area.

The buildings surrounding the two quadrangles of Wicklow College were either three or four stories high, and none had elevators. The senior faculty apartments, where David and I lived, were three stories, and Alice occupied a third-floor apartment across the stairway and above David.

"She liked the view," David said. "When her knee got so bad, the college offered to move her into a first-floor apartment, but she wouldn't have it."

I looked up and saw that all the apartments on that side had waist-high windows extending almost to the ceiling. I knew those upper windows provided a view of Wicklow City and the river to the north. The plunge from Alice's apartment to the sidewalk below was probably thirty or thirty-five feet. Yellow police tape presented a barrier we had to walk around, but we could see the chalk outline of where she came to rest and the blood stains on the sidewalk.

The body was gone, as were the police and the medical examiner's staff. I saw that the window was still open, with a curtain fluttering in the breeze, and felt sick. Maybe going to see that right after dinner wasn't a very good idea.

"That's a long way to fall," I said.

"Yes, and it looked as though she landed on her head and upper body," David said. "I heard the medical examiner say that death was probably instantaneous."

"When did either of you see her last?"

Kelly looked thoughtful, while David immediately said, "Yesterday. I was coming in from my afternoon class, and she was on her way to dinner at the Faculty Club. That was about four-fifteen, maybe four-thirty. She liked an early dinner, and she ate over there most of the time. With the faculty discount, it was cheaper than cooking at home—although I don't ever remember her cooking."

"It was last weekend," Kelly said. "I came over, and we worked on the book. It really is exciting in places. I finished up two chapters in the nineteen fifties. Her eyesight wasn't very good, so I would read it to her, and then we'd go through and edit it."

"And what was she doing in the fifties?" I asked.

"Sleeping with a lot of men in Berlin. Both sides of the Wall. It really will read like a spy novel."

"She didn't use a computer?" I asked.

Kelly shook her head. "Never learned to use one, at least according to her. There were a lot of things that she said she was too old to learn, but I'm not sure that was always true. When she wanted to, she was incredibly quick to pick up on things."

As we rounded the corner of the building and climbed the steps to the breezeway separating the two blocks of apartments, I heard noise from the construction of the bandstand on the Quad.

"What are you doing this weekend?" I asked.

"Me?" Kelly replied. "Going to Pittsburgh. My days of celebrating Samhain in Wicklow are over. I'm too old for that. A friend has tickets to a concert."

David chuckled. "I'm going fishing. I'm taking Lowell's spare room at his cabin."

"And no one invited me anywhere," I said, looking straight at David. He blushed and looked away, while Kelly had a coughing fit.

"Sorry. My friend isn't into threesomes," she said when she gained control again, and it was my turn to blush.

CHAPTER 3

Most universities mark time with their breaks—Thanksgiving, Christmas, New Year, Spring Break, Summer. At arcane colleges, the Solstices, Beltane, Samhain, Yule, and other solar and traditional holidays created additional short breaks that students treasured.

The funny thing was, the official celebrations of holidays and the student celebrations were often different. Take Samhain—or Halloween as it was more commonly called in the United States. In most colleges and universities, it was viewed with dread by the administrators and faculty. The students, on the other hand, looked forward to a huge party.

At Wicklow College of the Arcane Arts, the administration and faculty considered it an enormous party to be dreaded. It was an arcane event that contained an element of religion combined with terror.

Traditionally, The Celtic event of Samhain was a time when the veils between the real world and the world of the ancestors thinned, and the ancestors could cross—whether in their personas or simply to communicate.

It was my first Samhain at Wicklow, but I had experienced

the holiday at the Institute of Witchcraft on its various West Coast campuses for the past twenty years—several of those celebrations as a joyous student participant, and for the past dozen or so years, dreading it as a faculty member.

Of course, the college celebrations were usually rather mild in some aspects compared to the celebrations in Santa Fe, the center of the International Witches' Council, where I grew up. I had also attended the celebration in Scotland—the original site of the tradition—a couple of times as a teen. Not quite as wild as the Beltane celebration when I was sixteen, but the less said about that the better.

I assumed Professor Emeritus Henderson's untimely death the week before Samhain would add some spice to the event. I was sure most students had no idea she even existed, and most recent faculty, such as myself, were barely aware of her. But from the stories David and Kelly told me, it could be predicted that her legend would grow significantly. And of course, the possibility that her shade might cross the veil to reveal her killer definitely added a delightful shiver to the story.

Even though Samhain fell on a Wednesday, the students of Wicklow were not to be denied. The Friday night before, they partied until well after the bars closed.

My apartment was about as far as one could get from the dorms and Howard Quad—the center of the festivities—and still be on campus. I guessed the president's residence was more protected from the noise, but since I had no desire to take on the headaches of his position, or sample his bed, I was destined to remain ignorant.

I got up Saturday morning, ate breakfast, and caught the bus into town. After I had waited for weeks, my new bicycle arrived, and the idea of gaining some control over my mobility was one of the most exciting things that had happened to me since I arrived in Wicklow.

The woman I dealt with at the bike store had seemed to

understand what I wanted, and to my pleasant surprise, my new baby was everything I imagined. It had seven speeds to manage the hills in the area, a pretty wicker front basket, a rear luggage rack, and a trailer to haul groceries.

I had originally wanted it in black, but it was available only in cream color. Since I considered myself a white witch, I decided that was fine. I took it for a spin around town, and was quite satisfied when I pulled up in front of Carragher's Books and chained the bike to a parking meter.

The chain wasn't really necessary for security, but I figured I'd give casual passers-by a break. Bumping against the bike or the chain was harmless. Cutting the chain or the lock—or messing with the bike itself—would release a jolt of very unpleasant magic. Sort of like sticking a finger in an electrical socket.

Lowell Carragher was reading the latest bestseller from a young author in Ireland. He pretended to be engrossed and not paying attention to whomever walked in the door, but I caught a brief flash of his eyes turned toward me.

"Stop pretending to be intellectual," I said, leaning on the counter and giving him a smile. "Are you hiding porn or a comic book?"

He laughed and put the book down. "And how are you this pretty fall day, Savanna?"

"I'm wonderful. I got my new wheels. Want to come and see?"

I led him outside, and he walked around the bike, inspecting it.

"Have you named it yet?" he finally asked.

"Baby, because she's my baby, and I love her! I'm planning on riding her out to your resort for lunch. How come you're here? I thought you and David were going fishing."

"David went fishing. I'll join him tomorrow. Coffee or a cup of tea?"

We went back into the store, and he brewed me a cup of tea.

"I assume you heard about Alice Henderson?" I asked as I took a seat at the small table next to the counter.

He nodded. "Her death wasn't a surprise, given her age, but leaping out the window? I wouldn't have believed the old gal had it in her."

"How well did you know her?" I asked. Lowell knew almost everyone, and especially the Wicklow College faculty members.

"Better than most," he said. "She was one of my professors thirty years ago. A friend of my mother's."

"What do you think about her CIA stories?"

Lowell shrugged. "Any particular story you're interested in? I have no idea which of her stories were real, or which were embellished, but I do know she worked for the U.S. intelligence apparatus."

"I heard that you did, as well."

That got me a wink. "I had aspirations to be the American Ian Fleming, but I never got around to writing the books." He took a drink of his coffee. "I spent most of my Navy time in Latin America. Alice and I knew a lot of the same places, although she was retired and teaching here by the time I was stationed down there."

"Which places?"

"Argentina and southern South America, mostly. She knew a lot about the Falkland Islands, and she was there when the war between the UK and Argentina blew up. She owns a townhouse in Montevideo, Uruguay. At least, I think she still does. Did. She used to go down there in the summers when the college was out of session."

He got a faraway look, his hand lightly rubbing his chin.

"What?" I asked.

"Wondering who her heirs might be. That townhouse was nice."

"Don't you own enough?" In addition to the bookstore, a shopping center on the other side of the river, and half of a resort north of Wicklow City, I knew that Lowell owned at least three houses in various parts of the country.

He grinned. "I was thinking of a place for you. Have you thought at all what you'll do next summer? Hang around and go fishing with David and me?"

"Actually, I was planning on Spain and France."

"Too hot. You know, there's an old Irish proverb that says friends come and go, but enemies accumulate. The person you should talk to about Alice is Kelly Grace. You know she's writing a book about Alice, don't you?"

I nodded. "She asked me to proofread and format it before she sends it to the publisher. Well, thanks for the tea. I'm off to have lunch at your sister's place."

"Be careful. People around here don't pay enough attention to bicycles. Some of these idiots think the bicycle lanes are there so they can pass on the right."

"What good is witchcraft if you can't cast a shield spell around your bicycle?" I asked, giving him a smile and a wink.

I hadn't ridden a bike since leaving California two months before. I did use the university recreation center to swim regularly, and I had been riding their stationary bikes. But, after a twenty-mile ride into the country north of Wicklow City, my legs were screaming in pain. When I reached the resort and got off the bicycle, I wasn't sure my legs were going to hold me up.

Susan, Lowell's sister and the resort manager, came out on the lodge's porch and looked the bike over.

"Pretty fancy," she said. "I'm used to seeing mountain bikes, or motorcycles out here."

"Nope, this is urban transportation," I replied, taking my helmet off and shaking out my hair. "Maybe winter will convince me I need a car, but a bike similar to this provided everything I needed in San Francisco."

She laughed. "How many times did you get three feet of snow in San Francisco? Interested in some lunch?"

"That's what I came out for."

After a pleasant lunch with a glass of wine, I crawled back on the bike and headed back to town. My legs let me know I was over-doing it before I reached the main road.

I stopped at the grocery store and was in the middle of my shopping when I heard Kelly's voice behind me.

"Is Steven here?"

Usually, either Steve McCollum or Kelly gave me a ride to the store.

"No, I got my new bicycle. What are you doing here? I thought you were going to a concert in Pittsburgh."

Her face twisted into a very unhappy frown. "So did I. Sam Kagan hauled me into the police station for questioning, and I've been there all day."

"About?"

"Alice's death. They found my fingerprints in her apartment, so Kagan cooked up some fantasy about me murdering her. Now it's too late to make it to the concert."

"Yours weren't the only ones they found, were they?"

She shook her head. "They found David's on the outside of her door jamb, but none inside. They also found Sebastian Fernandez's prints in several places."

"Who's Sebastian Fernandez?"

"Her former brother-in-law. She hated him."

"Well, I guess we'll see if Kagan follows that clue."

We finished our shopping and left the store.

"That's an old lady bicycle," Kelly said, a frown on her face as she scrutinized my new pride and joy.

"I'm an old lady," I said as I loaded my groceries into the trailer. "Isn't this neat? No more bumming rides to the store."

"I'm sure you'll enjoy it in the rain, or this winter with snow and ice."

I shrugged. "The lady at the bike store said I can get chains, or even special winter snow tires. We'll see. So, did you satisfy Kagan, or are you still on his list?"

"I don't know. My prints are all over her place, and on the papers she and I worked with. He even tried to accuse me of trying to steal Alice's computer." Kelly's lips curled into an expression of distaste. "She didn't have a computer. Didn't know how to use one. I had one of the college's old laptops up at her place for me to use."

I finished strapping my boxes onto the trailer, then took my bike and walked with her over to where her car was parked.

"You may be next," Kelly said. "I overheard that they think Alice was drugged before she went out the window. The ME's report said they aren't sure what the drugs in her system were." She winked at me. "Sounds like an apothecarial conspiracy to me."

I watched her drive off, then rode to the college. I had already sweet-talked one of the maintenance men into installing a small bike rack next to my back door inside the walled herb garden. I parked the bike and locked it, disconnected the trailer, and locked it under the wooden stairs.

After hauling the groceries up to my apartment, I poured a hot bath to soak my poor aching legs. A glass of wine and a plate of cheese and fruit capped off a very fulfilling day.

CHAPTER 4

I answered a knock on the door to discover Lieutenant Sam Kagan holding a file folder.

"Dr. Robinson. Do you have a few minutes?"

"Certainly, Lieutenant. Come in. May I get you something to drink?"

"Oh, no, I'm fine."

He took a seat on the couch in my sitting room, and placed the file folder on the coffee table.

"We got the toxicology results on Alice Henderson," he said. "I was hoping you might take a look at them."

I sat down and opened the folder. "It seems pretty straightforward," I said after scanning results. "What did you find in the teacup?"

He cocked his head. "Who said anything about a teacup?"

"I just assumed that she drank this as a tea. Stomach contents included chamomile, sugar, lemon juice, peppermint, and valerian. A tea meant for helping someone to sleep, but not, I would think, for drinking in the middle of the afternoon. I assume it was ingested shortly before death, or it would have been completely absorbed."

"And the concentration of valerian?" he asked.

"Rather high, but not enough to knock someone out quickly. It could have been magically enhanced. The other ingredients were probably to hide the taste. Valerian is rather stinky and bitter. The Dilaudid they found in her blood is troubling. Did she have cancer?"

Kagan nodded. "Stage four pancreatic cancer. The ME said she probably only had a few weeks. How would you determine if magic was involved?"

I shook my head. "Very difficult. I would need to have the teacup while it was fairly fresh. Kelly Grace would probably be able to sense the magic better than I could. And of course, an analysis of stomach contents isn't going to be as accurate as having the original mixture."

"We didn't find any cups or glasses except in the cabinets. Nothing out on the tables or the kitchen counter."

"I suppose one could brew a potion or tincture and administer it that way. But you still have to get it in her. And the stomach content analysis indicates she drank something. Even a frail old woman would show some signs if the killer forced the potion into her mouth, don't you think?"

"You could concoct such a potion."

"As could my upper-level students." I waved in the direction of the college's herb garden outside my window. "We grow valerian, but I've seen it growing in yards in the city. Iris Bishop sells it in her shop. Lieutenant, it's been used since at least the Dark Ages. The oldest apothecary books I know of all include it."

Kagan didn't look happy.

I couldn't understand why someone would drug an old woman and toss her out the window. The cancer might make someone consider suicide, but from what I'd been told, she would have had a difficult time getting to and through the window. Especially all doped up.

"Lieutenant, do you have any motive for why someone might want to kill her?"

"There were papers in her apartment that someone might have been interested in."

"Other than the manuscript for the book she was working on with Kelly?"

He shrugged. "Well, thank you for your help."

I couldn't see as though I'd been much help. "I suppose someone could have given her some tea and taken the cup with them," I said. "In any case, it would seem she was killed by someone she knew."

Kagan nodded.

I saw him out, then brewed myself a cup of tea—without any valerian. A glance out my window revealed several strange-looking people wandering past. The Playboy bunny costume wouldn't have been out of place when I was a student. The dragon costume was quite inventive and well done. The beer bottles both of them were carrying promised that the evening would not be quiet and relaxing.

It was well before dark, but I heard a rock band start to play on Howard Quad, and I realized that I needed to find a place to hide out for the evening.

I made a couple of calls. Since Kelly had missed her concert, I thought she might like to go out for dinner, and Steven's apartment overlooked Howard Quad, where the band would be playing. Both agreed a trip back out to Carragher's Retreat sounded like a good idea.

※

"A large dose of valerian and throw her out the window. Gee, that's subtle," Steven said in response to me telling my friends about Lieutenant Kagan's visit. We were in Kelly's car, driving out to Carragher's.

"As far as I know, Alice didn't have any trouble sleeping," Kelly said. "She did have arthritis and often used a magically enhanced tincture of willow bark, turmeric, and ginger in either green tea or single malt scotch."

Steven chuckled. "Maybe the scotch was why she didn't have any sleep problems."

When we entered the dining room, Susan smiled at me. "So good you couldn't stay away?"

"You're not celebrating Samhain with kegs of beer and a bad rock band are you?"

"Thankfully not," she replied. "Lowell's here and eating alone," she suggested with a questioning expression.

"Sure, let's go bother him," I said.

Susan led us to where Lowell was sitting at the table with the best view overlooking the river.

"We heard you were having a quiet dinner," I said. "You spend too much time alone."

"Probably," he said with a smile. "Won't you join me?"

Lowell was halfway through his dinner, and I encouraged him to continue eating while the rest of us perused the menu and Susan brought another bottle of wine.

We lingered after dinner, but after dropping Kelly at her house, Steven and I still got back to the college well before the festivities wound down. I pitied him since his apartment overlooked the craziness in Howard Quad. We said good night, and he continued toward his place.

As I closed my door, I caught a movement across the breezeway and peered through a crack in the door. Someone was coming toward me, trying to stay in the shadows. I was able to tell that it was a man when he opened the door to the stairs that led to David's and Alice's apartments. Since neither was home, I continued to watch for a while. After about ten minutes, I detected a faint glow through the curtains of Alice's apartment. Fifteen minutes later, the glow disappeared, and shortly thereafter, the man came out the door and crept back toward Howard Quad.

I considered calling Lieutenant Kagan and telling him about the intruder, but it was late, the man had gone, and I seriously doubted he had left any clues Kagan would be able to find. The band and the shouting from that direction were still very loud. I cast a shield for silence and went to bed.

CHAPTER 5

A couple of days after Samhain, I met Kelly at the Faculty Club for lunch. She sat down and immediately launched into a rant about the police.

"Kagan won't release any of the papers in Alice's apartment. Not only that, but they evidently found some sort of diary or journal that I didn't know existed. He won't even let me look at it."

"You said she deposited some papers at the library under a spell lock," I said. "Have you looked at those?" Normally, a witch's spells dissolved upon their death.

She nodded. "Dr. Phillips and I opened them yesterday afternoon." Edmund Phillips was the college president and Kelly's boss. "We sort of sifted through them, just to get a gist of what was there. A lot of it is about the time she spent in South America, and we found her will."

"Oh? And how interesting was that?"

Kelly shrugged. "I didn't get a good look at it, and Edmund took it. Said he was going to give it to the college's lawyer."

"It would be interesting to see who might benefit from her death," I said.

She shook her head. "Don't go playing detective again. Last time you did that, someone tried to kill you."

"Funny you should mention that. After you dropped me off the other night, I saw someone go into Alice's rooms. I don't know who, other than I think it was a man."

That got me an eye roll. "Did you tell Kagan?"

"No. What would he do with the information? Learn to lock the door?" In a previous murder investigation at the college, Kelly and I discovered that the police had failed to secure the apartment where the killing had taken place.

"You haven't been in her apartment, have you?" Kelly asked.

"I wouldn't go in without you. I've never been in there."

"If Kagan caught us, he'd throw a fit. Besides, from the hints he dropped, they've taken every scrap of paper out of there, and her papers are all I'm interested in."

"I think it would be interesting to see the scene. You and David have been in her apartment, and you both seem convinced that she couldn't have jumped. But I've never seen the place."

"Unless she had help, or moved the table and had a step stool, she never could have gotten onto the window sill in the living room," Kelly said. "It would have been easier for her to go out the bedroom window."

I was a little jealous. My bedroom lacked a window due to a two-story concrete laboratory building next to my apartment.

"So, what were the papers locked away in the library about?" I asked.

"Mostly about her time in South America. I guess she really did work for the CIA. And some of them concern her family. Her half-sister grew up in Argentina and married a guy there. The papers are a combination of her recollections, letters to and from her sister and her sister's kids, and copies of reports to her CIA bosses, along with a bunch of documents. It's going to take some time to go through and catalog them all."

"I wonder why she would be locking some of that away."

"Probably because copying those reports was against the rules," Kelly said. "My dad never made copies of his reports and shredded any working papers."

※

Kelly always parked her car near my apartment, and the following day she stopped by after she got off work.

"Want to hear the latest on Alice?" she asked when I answered the door.

"Sure. Glass of wine?"

I led her into the sitting room, then pulled a bottle of red and two glasses from the kitchen.

"Edmund told me that Alice's will leaves everything to her niece and nephew, including her share of the proceeds from the book once I publish it," Kelly started. "The lawyer is still trying to trace all her assets, so no idea how extensive they are."

"Lowell told me she owns a place in Uruguay," I said.

Kelly shrugged. "I had some time today to sort through the papers she archived at the library. A couple of surprises. Have you met Sebastian Fernandez? He teaches life magic."

I shook my head. "No, I know about him only from your comments."

"Did I tell you that he's Alice's ex-brother-in-law? And her papers contain a case pointing to him as the murderer of his wife, Alice's half-sister."

"No kidding?"

She nodded. "There's a lot about the sister's death. She fell off a cliff while on holiday with Sebastian. Officially, it was ruled an accident, but evidently Alice never believed it."

Kelly went on to tell me that Alice's father had died when she was young. Her mother returned to South America and married the heir of an old Argentine family that owned a prosperous vineyard and winery. They had a daughter, Camila, who inherited the business when her parents were killed in a plane crash.

I thought that it already sounded like a novel.

Camila married a man named Carlos Arias, and they had twins. Carlos was killed when the twins were very young, and soon after, Camila married Sebastian Fernandez.

Then Camila was killed in a fall from a third-floor balcony. Alice had been entrusted with Camila's will, but Sebastian and the winery's lawyer produced a later will. Instead of leaving the business to Camila's children, the newer will left everything to Sebastian.

Alice had a fit, contesting the will, filing lawsuits on the children's behalf, and accusing Sabastian of his wife's murder. She evidently lost, and in the end, Sabastian walked away with the business and all the money.

"And he ended up teaching here at Wicklow College?" I asked.

Kelly pursed her lips. "I guess he sold the vineyard and moved here. Alice followed him, applied for a teaching position, and was hired the following year. She's been keeping an eye on him ever since."

Such a tangled set of relationships. Even more complicated than my situation when I was growing up. I wondered how such families kept it all straight. "I guess we should put him at the top of the suspects' list, don't you think?"

"She definitely planned on using this material in the book. I'm going to talk to Edmund about it tomorrow. I wonder if he knew they had a previous relationship."

"How old is Fernandez?" I asked.

"Around his sixties, I'd guess."

"And the kids? The nephew and niece?"

"In their early forties. I assume the lawyer will be contacting them about the will. I'd love the chance to talk with them if they come here."

"How many people knew you planned to publish this book?" I asked.

"The book isn't a secret. When I signed the publishing contracts last year, it got quite a bit of local publicity."

"You already have a publisher?"

"Two actually. There will be a straight version leaving out the magic, and another version including the magic. The advances add up to six-figures. One of Alice's old lovers works at a big New York publishing house."

"Do you know if any of her old employers were concerned?"

Kelly laughed. "Not that I know of. James Bond hasn't been around to see me, in any case."

CHAPTER 6

If I had lived out in the woods someplace, I would have made my own candles. But since Wicklow City was only two miles away, and Iris Bishop's boutique only a few blocks farther, I rode my bike into town the Saturday after Kelly told me about Alice's family.

Back to Basics sold witchcraft tools and accessories, herbs, and other ingredients, as well as charms, potions, and tinctures. It also sold a lot of touristy stuff. Iris had inherited the business when her sister was killed, and was still making changes to fit her own vision.

I locked the bike to a parking meter out front, and went in. The smell of incense and herbs, along with the lighting, immediately set an atmosphere of witchy spookiness.

"Savanna! How nice to see you. How did you survive Samhain out at the college?" Iris greeted me. She was a thin, pretty woman about my age—early forties—with light brown hair pulled back in a ponytail, wearing a smock and faded blue jeans.

"I escaped out to Carragher's Retreat and used a silence spell when I got home," I said.

"I could hear that band all the way here," Iris said. "Weren't they terrible?"

I shrugged. "I think the band members are students. I hope they do better at their studies than they do with their instruments. I came in to get some candles."

She showed me her selection, and I picked out a couple of dozen black ones. I needed them for my students to use for an alchemy lesson, and black was always more impressive when working magic.

Afterward, I rode over to Kelly's house. I was surprised to see Lieutenant Kagan's slightly beat-up car and a couple of marked police cars parked in front of her house.

I locked my bike to her front-porch railing and peeked through the screen door. Kelly sat in a chair in the living room, and Kagan sat across from her on the couch.

"Am I interrupting anything important?" I called.

Kagan opened his mouth to say something, but Kelly was faster, causing the cop to frown.

"Come on in."

Since I'm naturally nosey, I did.

"What's up?" I asked.

Again, Kelly beat the cop. "Someone tried to break into my house this morning. Just before dawn."

"Aren't you warded?" I asked.

"Oh, yeah, but whoever it was tested my wards."

So, a witch.

"An ardent admirer, or someone interested in Alice's papers?" I asked.

"That's what the lieutenant asked."

"I'm just trying to get the whole story," he said, an exasperated expression on his face.

"Oh, sorry." I took a seat. "I'll keep quiet."

After half an hour, Kagan ran out of questions and left.

"There was a footprint—a man's shoe—in the flowerbed by the

spare bedroom," Kelly said after he left. I knew her spare bedroom served mostly as her home office. "They took a plaster cast of it."

"You didn't see him?"

She shook her head. "I woke up when he tested the wards, but by the time I got out of bed and went to look, he was gone. I called the cops, and it took them forever to get here."

"I hope you're not in danger."

"After Alice's death, I renewed all my wards, and I carry my wand everywhere I go. Until we figure out what's going on, I'm going to be extra careful."

A knock on my door the following morning revealed a very handsome mid-thirtyish man in a business suit. He was dressed far more nicely than our local detectives, and definitely different than the khakis and tweed jackets worn by most of the college professors.

"Ms. Robinson?" he asked in a silky baritone. Since there was a plaque next to my door with my name on it, he'd made a good guess.

"Dr. Robinson, yes," I replied.

"I'm Jefferson Colby." He flashed an identity card. The only thing I read on it were the words, 'Central Intelligence Agency.'

"Good morning. How can I help the government?"

"I'm investigating the death of Alice Henderson. May I come in?"

I shrugged. "I'm afraid there isn't much I can tell you. I wasn't home at the time, and I've already spoken to the campus and local police."

"I understand you're friends with Kelly Grace."

"We are colleagues."

"May I come in?"

It was a gray and blustery day, the temperature cold enough for a heavier coat than he was wearing. I didn't really want to talk to him, let alone welcome him into my home.

"I was just getting ready to go out," I said.

His expression told me he didn't plan to take the hint. His only movement was to lean toward me. "It won't take very long."

I stepped out of the way, pulling the door open. He walked in and proceeded down the short hallway to my sitting room, where he stood and looked around. I judged him to be a little over six feet, with broad shoulders. The suit was obviously tailored to his athletic build. His light brown hair was short and neatly trimmed.

"Please have a seat," I said, indicating the couch. I sat in a chair with the coffee table between us.

He held out his hand and sparked a flame in the middle of his palm. It danced around a bit, then he snuffed it.

"I'm with the Supernatural Investigations Unit of the agency's Operations Directorate," he said.

Something about him really irritated me, and his little demonstration only added to it.

"A witchy spook. Or is it a spooky witch?" I held out my palm and kindled a flame like a blowtorch. I let it burn for a moment, then closed my hand. "I'm a professor of alchemy and apothecary. How can I help you?"

He'd made the mistake of looking into that white-hot flame, and sat back, blinking rapidly.

Once he regained his composure, he said, "You once worked as an investigator for the Witches' Council."

"A long time ago. I investigated financial issues, corporate issues. I wasn't a covert operative or a criminal investigator."

"Well, I'm the agency's liaison to the Witches' Council's enforcement arm."

"Congratulations. Agent Colby, is there a point to this? I'll be honest, I'm not interested in your resume."

"As I said, I'm investigating the death of Alice Henderson."

"And as *I* said, I know nothing about it."

He straightened and took a deep breath. "We understand that your friend, Kelly Grace, is in possession of a number of classified documents Alice unlawfully kept when she left the agency."

I shrugged. "You'll have to talk to Kelly about that. I haven't seen any such thing."

"I was hoping you might persuade her to be a little more cooperative. I'd hate to think of her going to jail."

And I normally would hate to see a person turned into a toad, but Agent Colby was rapidly beating down my ethical barriers. I wondered if there might be such a spell in my grimoire.

"I would hate to see anyone get hurt," I said. "Perhaps you should try negotiating a little better. Now, if that's all, I'm on my way to the gym."

I stood, indicating that our chat was over. He reluctantly also stood, and I followed him to the door.

"Good day, Mr. Colby. I hope you have better luck on your next assignment."

After I closed the door, I called Kelly and told her about my visitor.

"Yeah, he came to see me. Threatened me. I called my editor, who called their lawyers. The CIA has a reputation of trying to stop publication of anything they think might be embarrassing, whether it has to do with national security or not."

CHAPTER 7

That evening, I heard a knock at my door. Normally, I didn't have a lot of visitors, so I was surprised to find another stranger wanting to see me.

"Dr. Robinson? I am Tomas Ortiz," the elderly gentleman in a white suit said with an Argentine accent. "I was a friend of Alice Henderson's."

"¿Cómo está usted?" I responded.

"Quite well, thank you. I believe you know my nephew, Diego."

"I did. How may I help you?"

I had worked with Diego Ortiz once in Buenos Aires, almost twenty years before, when I was with the Witches' Council. The relationship had evolved—temporarily—into something a bit more than professional. I knew Diego's uncle by reputation.

Señor Ortiz had bushy white hair and a mustache that contrasted with his brown skin. He was stooped a bit, as older people often were, and leaned on a cane. I reached out with my magic and confirmed that the cane was a magic wand.

"I would like to speak with you about Alice, if I may."

I invited him in and fixed tea and a plate of cookies.

"I was the inspector who investigated Camila Fernandez's death," he began. "Along with Alice, I never believed it was an accident, but I was unable to prove otherwise. I understand that the police are having the same trouble with Alice's death."

"I assume so," I said. "I haven't spoken to the police in a while, but there seem to be circumstances that make either an accident or suicide difficult to accept."

He nodded.

"It happened here?" he asked. "I was told her flat was across the breezeway."

"That's true, but the actual scene of her death was on the other side of the building."

"Do you know if the police have questioned Sebastian Fernandez?"

I shook my head. "I don't. I'm not sure they know his connection to Alice."

"But you do."

"Only because of references found in documents I was told about after her death."

"I see. Do you know how I can contact a woman named Kelly Grace? I understand she was working with Alice on her memoir."

I didn't see any harm in giving him Kelly's number since I planned on warning her as soon as Ortiz left. We chatted a little more, and then he took his leave. I couldn't figure out how he knew where to find me but didn't know how to contact Kelly?

I called Kelly immediately, and she said, "I think it's interesting that all these people are coming out of the woodwork on Alice's death, and it all seems to tie into Argentina. I would have thought the CIA would be as concerned about her time in Germany and Russia. But the only concerns Colby mentioned were about South America."

She paused, then said, "You don't suppose the CIA was responsible for her death, do you?"

"I think it shouldn't be ruled out. They've done their homework if they're trying to use our friendship to get to you through me. We've only known each other about ten weeks."

I briefly considered trying to call Diego to confirm the old man's story but wasn't sure that he—or his wife—would appreciate my contacting him. He wasn't married when I knew him, but as I was leaving Argentina, I found out that he was engaged. His fiancée had shown up to see me off at the airport, and it wasn't cordial.

I contented myself with an internet search, followed by searches on the witches' web, and what the old man had told me checked out. The pictures of Tomas Ortiz that I found showed a man twenty years younger than the man at my door.

Similar searches on Colby found nothing about him on the open internet, which didn't surprise me. On the witches' web, I didn't find much, and all of it was prior to his college graduation. When I used my own accesses to tap into the Council databases, he did appear. He wasn't in the Council's best graces, and his loyalty to his employer seemed to far outweigh his loyalty to his family and other magic users.

It wasn't that the Council and mundane governments had an adversarial relationship, but any serious student of political history was aware that one-tenth of one percent of the population had fought the rest of Europe to a standstill in the twelfth through eighteenth centuries. The crater where Rome used to be was a reminder of how that turned out. The British Empire had never recovered from Cromwell's invasion of Scotland. Events in Asia followed a similar path. Witches and mundanes still viewed each other with suspicion.

I went to the college recreation center, worked out, and then took a swim. Back at my apartment, I changed clothes and went to dinner at the Faculty Club.

On my way home, I glanced up at Alice's apartment and saw a light on. There were also lights on in David's apartment below hers. I hesitated, but my curiosity got the best of me. Drawing my wand, I entered the stairwell leading to their apartments.

David answered his door when I knocked. He was barefoot, wearing a pair of sweat pants and a t-shirt—not at all the semi-formal slacks and jacket that were his normal attire. I knew that he tried to keep himself in shape, and the t-shirt hugged his torso, showing off his toned upper body.

"Savanna?" His brow creased in bewilderment. In two months of knowing him, I had never been in his place.

"There's a light on in Alice's window," I said.

"Oh, no. You're not going up there."

"Not alone. Put some shoes on."

He stared at me for a long minute, then sighed. He sat down on a stool there in his foyer and pulled on a pair of soft-soled shoes.

"Let me get my wand," he said, standing and going into his rooms. I waited for him.

David was an elemental witch, adept at manipulating air, water, fire, and earth. I had never seen him use his magic, but Kelly had taken classes from him when she was a student. He had a solid reputation among the faculty.

"I'll go first," he said, brushing past me onto the landing.

I didn't argue. Physically, he was much larger than I was, and I was somewhat fearful of who we might find upstairs.

We reached Alice's door, and David tried the knob.

"Locked."

I waved him aside and spelled the lock, which opened with

a soft click. He gave me an expressionless glance, then turned the knob, and slowly pushed the door inward.

We hesitated in the foyer. A glow from the bedroom—the window I had seen—was the only light in the apartment. Cautiously, David moved forward, and I followed him.

A quick search found no one there but us. I created a dim mage light and set it on my shoulder. David did the same.

I looked around and saw the window Alice had fallen out of. A side table against the wall under the window was about as wide and high as a kitchen counter. It would have been an effort for *me* to climb on that table to reach the window, let alone for a gimpy woman in her eighties.

The place was a mess. Every cabinet, every drawer had been opened and emptied. The bed had been stripped of the covers, and the mattress had been turned over. All the clothes in the closet were lying on the floor, and all the shoe boxes were open. Most of the surfaces were covered with fingerprint dust, and the dust had been disturbed in a lot of places. I looked closely at a handprint on the frame of the bedroom closet and couldn't see any fingerprints. The person who left it had been wearing gloves.

"Was the place ransacked when the police came in?" I asked.

David shook his head. "I don't think so. Sam Kagan didn't say anything about it. Your late-night prowler who left the light on, perhaps?"

There was a sound at the outside door, and I whirled around, raising my wand to defend myself.

"And what are you doing here?" Lieutenant Kagan asked. He had his pistol in his hand. A uniformed cop stood in the doorway behind him.

"We saw a light on in the bedroom," I said.

"And didn't think to call me?"

"Sorry. We came up here and the door was open."

He glared at me, then holstered his gun, and triggered the mage lights in the main room.

"Somebody's been doing some rearranging," he said, looking around.

"I've had a couple of visitors, looking for Alice's papers," I said.

The lieutenant walked to the bedroom and peered in.

"Looks like I should set some wards on the place. Locks certainly haven't been effective."

"I'm not sure there's any point," David said. "I doubt whoever did this will be back. Why are you here?"

"One of your neighbors did think calling the police was a good idea when they saw the light."

"Damned busybodies," I remarked and Kagan snorted.

"Have you made any progress on the investigation?" David asked.

"I spent this afternoon telling a federal agent how little progress we've made." Kagan said. "He wanted me to confiscate Kelly's book and turn it over to him."

"I'm so going to buy that book," I said.

Kagan grinned. "Me, too. A lawyer for her publisher will be in town tomorrow. The publisher used a local lawyer to file an injunction against touching anything she has. I'm pretty sure the judge will tell her she has to show Alice's papers to me, but I'll be shocked if he rules in the government's favor."

I wandered over to the window Alice had exited through.

"The window was open?" I asked. "I didn't see any glass outside."

He shook his head. "It was open, and I've ruled out suicide. She had bruises from someone's hands on her upper arms."

I shuddered. "How terrifying that must have been."

Both men nodded.

Kagan showed us out, locked the door, then sketched runes

on the doorframe with a marker, and cast a ward. Kagan was a witch, but not a particularly strong or knowledgeable one. I paid attention to the spell he cast, and was pretty sure I could undo it and recast it.

CHAPTER 8

I called Kelly the following morning and invited her to lunch at the Faculty Club. When she arrived, I told her of my foray into Alice's apartment the previous evening.

She shook her head. "I can't believe this has gotten so far out of hand. That guy, Colby, is a real piece of work. He went from imploring me to abandon the book out of patriotism to threatening me with prosecution for revealing government secrets. Savanna, what possible damage could I do to national security by writing about Alice's love affairs fifty years ago?"

"They don't care about national security," I said, "they're worried about embarrassment. The U.S. doesn't want to admit they fielded spies with loose morals."

Kelly laughed. "Such as Jefferson Colby? I'm fairly sure part of his magic has to do with psychological manipulation. He was definitely trying to spell me when we met, and he was soooo disappointed when it didn't work."

"A coercion spell?" Such spells were banned by the Witches' Council.

"Yeah, and more subtle ones as well. There might have been a seduction spell in there, too."

"He didn't try anything like that on me. Maybe he didn't think I was worth the effort."

"Probably intimidated. Hard to reconcile the concept of a dumb blonde with a woman who has two doctorates."

I snorted. "If he was intimidated, it was more likely by my father." I was sure Colby's intelligence about me included that my dad was a member of the Council. I didn't mind being protected from politics by the association.

Another thought struck me. "Wasn't she in South America during a time when they were doing revolutions and things like that?"

Kelly's eyes shifted to somewhere past my shoulder. I twisted in my seat, trying to see what interested her.

"Sebastian Fernandez," she said.

I had looked up his picture on the Wicklow College web, but it took me a moment to recognize him. The picture must have been very old. The picture also didn't convey how huge he was. Even with him seated, I could tell he was very tall, and very fat. His face and head were shaven smooth. He sat several tables away from us, busy with demolishing a huge, bloody steak.

"He's certainly large enough to throw Alice through a window," I said.

"He's large enough to throw David out the window," Kelly answered. She was probably right, even though David Hamilton was rather large himself—six feet and probably two hundred pounds.

I studied Fernandez out of the corner of my eye. He wore a gray suit, the collar of his white shirt open with no tie.

"You said he teaches life magic?" I asked.

"Yes. He's not a healer, though. Quite the opposite, in fact. He manipulates life energy—plants or animals. I had one class with him, and found him to be rather distasteful. He bullies and intimidates students."

"Lovely."

"He told me once that my looks wouldn't help my grade. Pissed me off, and I got a top mark in his class."

"Rather unprofessional."

"He sucks up to Edmund, though. Typical bully."

"Did you ever talk to him about Alice's accusations?"

She shook her head. "I haven't had the chance."

There was so much mystery about Alice Henderson's death, and it distracted me from my classes. I found myself spending a lot of time on the computer reading the history surrounding her life and work for the government.

It also bothered me that a second faculty murder—in only six months—had occurred in the apartment block where I lived. Everyone said the deaths were an anomaly, but I was starting to feel very unsafe.

I had just come home after my last class of the day and was pouring myself a glass of wine when the phone rang. "Savanna?" David Hamilton's voice. "The police have arrested Kelly. Would you like to go with me to bail her out?"

"What? On what charge?"

"Murder. Some guy that she found dead in her yard, from what I can gather. She called me because a friend of mine here in town is a lawyer."

"Sure, I'll come. I'm ready right now. Do I need to bring a checkbook?"

"That part is already taken care of."

We found Kelly sitting in the lobby of the police station, and she was hopping mad. As soon as three of us got in David's car, she let loose a stream of language I had never heard her use, all directed at Sam Kagan.

"You'll have to take me to your place," she said when she finally wound down. "My house has been declared a crime scene, and Lieutenant Kagan is taking full advantage by confiscating all of my papers, computer, and anything else that in his judgement might be connected to Alice Henderson."

"What happened?" I asked.

"I found Jefferson Colby dead in my garden," she said. "The first thing Kagan did when the cops showed up was arrest me."

I offered to let her sleep on my couch, but she declined. She had a room with a bed off her office at the library where she sometimes slept when she worked late.

"But I would appreciate it if I could drop by for breakfast and a shower in the morning," she said.

"He was just lying there dead?" David asked. "Any indications as to how he died?"

Kelly shook her head. "I heard a noise outside, and went to investigate. He was lying there, and I couldn't see any blood or anything. He just had a shocked expression on his face. My lawyer said he would try and find out something more tomorrow."

After we dropped Kelly off at the library, I rode with David to park his car.

"No signs of what killed him probably makes Kagan think it was magic," I said.

David nodded. "Yes, but we'll see what the autopsy shows. The chief medical examiner is a witch, so I'm sure she'll look for the kind of damage magic might do."

"Unless someone used fire or lightning, it would be hard to tell," I said. "A wielder of life magic or a healer could just stop someone's heart."

"Didn't you say that Colby was a witch? He should have been able to shield himself."

"Not if the other person was much stronger than he was. The thing is, we're assuming there were two people prowling around outside her house. Who was the second one? She had a prowler a few days ago, and reported it to the police. They came and sniffed around, but nothing came of it."

"And Kagan is probably thinking that she took matters into her own hands this time," David said.

When Kelly came for breakfast, she said, "I need to go shopping. I don't have anything to wear, and they won't let me in my house. To make things worse, I don't even have my car keys."

I looked her over and knew I couldn't lend her anything. She was too tall and I was too curvy for anything of mine to fit her.

"I'll call Steven," I said. Steven McCollum was the greenhouse manager and a former student of mine in California. He was gay, with an excellent fashion sense. He came over about half an hour later.

"I haven't taken a woman shopping since I moved to Wicklow," he said with a grin. "I can use the practice."

Since his car was a two-seat sports car, I couldn't go with them, but I had a class to teach anyway. So, I gave Kelly the extra key to my apartment and went on about my day.

That afternoon, I came home to find her lawyer knocking on my door. Myron Overton was a fishing buddy of David's, and the top criminal lawyer in Wicklow.

Overton looked like a lawyer. Expensive suit, widow's peak, and gray at the temples, with an air of stuffy seriousness.

"Is Kelly here?" he asked.

I told him that she probably was still at the library. I let him in and offered him some tea or coffee, but he just asked for a glass of water. He put his briefcase on the floor and sat with a whoosh of breath.

"It's been a day, and I have some news," Myron said. "They completed the autopsy on Agent Colby, and all they found was a bruise on his left cheek. That could have happened when he fell, or shortly before that. In any case, the ME said it occurred shortly before he died. Her speculation is a heart attack, possibly caused by magic, but no way to prove it. Lieutenant Kagan is calling in an investigator from the Witches' Council."

He shifted in his seat. "The other news is that a team of government people flew in from Washington. They can't take over the investigation, since the CIA is prohibited from operations in the U.S., but they've made it very clear they're going to be looking over the shoulders of the local police."

I heard the front door open, and Kelly came in. She looked at the two of us, and directed her attention to Overton. He repeated what he'd told me about the autopsy.

"What about all the papers and computers they confiscated?" Kelly asked. "They can't just take all that, can they?"

He shook his head. "They're trying to find motive, and that's all they have. I'll file a motion with the court to drop the charges tomorrow. If he wasn't murdered, then they have no grounds to arrest you. I'll also petition the court to get your stuff back, but I wouldn't hold my breath. They'll probably keep it until after the trial, or until the charges are dropped."

Kelly shrugged. "No big deal. I have copies and backups of everything. But this is ridiculous. What motive would I have for killing him?"

"If you did, I'd be pleading self-defense," Myron said. "Since you didn't, I have no idea what the police are thinking."

"He was a very irritating man," I said. "If she did, we would have hidden the body instead of calling Kagan."

Myron chuckled. "Please don't say things like that in front of Sam Kagan."

CHAPTER 9

The people from the CIA lost no time in showing up at my door. Two men dressed almost identically to Jefferson Colby flashed their IDs when I answered their knock.

"Kelly Grace?" the one with light brown hair asked.

"No. I'll call her."

"May we come in?"

"No."

I shut the door and went to retrieve Kelly from the kitchen.

"Two spooks from the CIA are here to see you. Unless they have a warrant, I'm inclined to let them stand outside."

She looked out the window, then gave me a faint smile. "Weather's kinda nasty."

"Yes. Hopefully it will discourage them."

Kelly went to the door and opened it. I trailed behind.

"I'm Kelly Grace."

They went through the ritual of showing her their IDs and introducing themselves.

"May we come in?"

"Not without a warrant. And besides, my lawyer has advised me not to speak with anyone."

"Miss Grace, surely you understand that it's in your best interest to cooperate."

She gave them a patronizing smile. "I'm just a dumb blonde. I don't understand anything about this whole mess."

And with that, she shut the door in their faces. I burst out laughing.

"I spoke with my father last night," Kelly said, "and he said I have zero obligation to help them out. Colby should never have been here in the first place. The CIA is completely out of their lane on this one. If they want Alice's papers, the proper approach would have been to have one of their lawyers contact me or my publisher."

"And a judge would deny them for prior restraint," I said. "I saw a few government coverups when I worked for the Council. They always try and scare people into cooperating when they don't have a legal leg to stand on."

"And the Council never does such things?" she asked.

"The Witches' Council is a form of government," I answered.

She called her lawyer and told him of the visit. He said she had done exactly the correct thing.

Our next visit, the following day, was from a woman in a neatly tailored suit carrying a briefcase. Her brown hair flowed loosely over her shoulders, almost to her waist. She looked familiar, but at first I couldn't place her.

"Dr. Robinson, I'm Kathleen Furman. We met at a reception in Santa Fe a few years ago. I understand that Kelly Grace is staying with you?"

"You're with the Council?" I asked.

"Yes."

I didn't invite her in, either. I called Kelly, who was in the living room reading through some of Alice's documents using a college computer.

"Woman from the Witches' Council," I said.

"Wonderful. Savanna, I've been combing through all this stuff of Alice's, and there's nothing I can see that would be of national security interest. Hell, most of the people she mentions are dead now."

She got up and went to the front door. Her conversation with Furman wasn't much longer than the one with the CIA. She came back and dropped into her chair.

"Colby's death is getting a lot more attention than Alice's," she said. "If they put this much attention on solving her murder, instead of leaving it to Kagan, they might make some progress."

"Which tells me they are more worried about her papers being an embarrassment than a security issue," I said. "She didn't have any relationships with people who were high up in the government, did she? Senators, Cabinet secretaries, that sort of thing?"

Kelly winked at me. "A few. Mostly dead now. But I can't see a senator showing up twenty years later and throwing her out a window."

"I could see someone in power asking a favor—say of an old friend in the CIA—and having an underling get overzealous."

"That would sell more books than the original affair. People love conspiracies."

"If they ever catch who killed her."

Kelly leaned back in her chair, a thoughtful look on her face.

"Suppose we have this all wrong?" she asked. "What if her murder had nothing to do with the book?"

"A jealous wife tracked her down forty years later?" I replied. "Or maybe she was selling magical drugs to the students and failed to pay her supplier?"

"Yeah, motive is an issue, isn't it?"

"Maybe her long-abandoned love child tracked her down."

My friend shook her head. "I think she always wanted a child. Three miscarriages. She got very morose when she talked about them."

THE REVENGE GAME

The following morning on my way to class, I discovered one of the CIA agents waiting for me at the end of the breezeway leading to the Quad.

"Dr. Robinson," he said, stepping in front of me. "May I speak to you for a moment?"

"I can spare only a moment. I'm on my way to class."

He nodded. "I was hoping you might convince your friend, Miss Grace, to be a little more cooperative. All we want is her agreement to allow us to review her book before it's published. I'm sure you understand that issues of national security are at stake here."

I shrugged. "I'm sure your lawyers have a case to make through the normal legal channels."

"That would be costly and delay her. Surely, you can help us to make her see reason."

He suddenly reached out and grabbed me by my upper arms.

"She needs to understand who she's dealing with."

I muttered a shock spell, and he stumbled backwards.

"You need to keep your hands to yourself," I said. "I won't press charges for assault this time, but this is your only warning."

"Bitch!"

I grinned. "Idiot. Run along and keep away from me. You're lucky that I'm feeling charitable this morning. Catch me in a bad mood, and I'll hurt you."

It turned out to be my day for fools. Alice's ex-brother-in-law, Sebastian Fernandez, was waiting for me at the base of the steps to the Administration Building.

"Dr. Robinson?" he called as I walked past him.

I turned to face him. "Yes?"

"I understand that you've been approached by Tomas Ortiz.

I should warn you that he is a very deranged man. He is full of crazy ideas. Discredited ideas. His irrational hatred of me almost derailed his career in Argentina years ago, and now he's here, trying to spread lies about me in the wake of Alice's death. I hope you will keep an open mind. Alice and I worked here for decades without any animosity, but now Ortiz seems to want to stir things up with unfounded allegations. Miss Grace would be very mistaken to listen to his ravings."

"I shall keep that in mind," I said. "Now, I have a class to teach, if you'll please excuse me."

Interesting. He didn't introduce himself, but assumed I knew who he was. He also knew about my discussion with Ortiz. And why did everyone assume I could tell Kelly what to do?

I asked her that when we met for lunch—more as a rhetorical question than expecting to get an answer.

"Probably because you're older than I am, and they think you'll see reason and lend me your mature wisdom. I'm young and hot-headed, ya know?"

I had to laugh. "That would be the first time anyone has accused me of mature wisdom."

"Edmund told me this morning that Alice's niece and nephew will be coming in tomorrow," Kelly said.

"Have the lawyers nailed down all her assets?" I asked.

"My understanding is yes. Her estate isn't very large, and it all goes to them, split equally."

"Quite a come-down from inheriting a successful vineyard," I said.

Kelly nodded. "I also came across something I don't understand. I hadn't paid much attention to it when I first went through the documents she had sealed in the library. I made a copy of it."

She handed me a single piece of paper, densely covered in

handwritten numbers, letters, and symbols. It took me a couple of minutes to make any sense of it.

"It's the key to some kind of code," I said. "You just have to find the encoded document to translate it."

"And how am I supposed to recognize that? Almost everything she had is written in English or Spanish, but there are a few things written in German or Russian. I'll have to find a translator for the ones that aren't in English. Did you know that printed Russian and cursive handwriting look totally different?"

CHAPTER 10

The evening Alice's heirs arrived, Kelly invited me to dinner at the Faculty Club with them.

"Have you met them yet?" I asked as we waited for them.

"Briefly. Edmund sent a car to pick them up at the airport, and I met them before they went to their hotel." She shrugged. "Long enough to invite them to dinner."

"Are they staying at the Wayfarer's Inn?"

"Of course. The college has a deal there."

"What have they been told?"

"I have no idea. They know their aunt is dead, they are named in her will, and that I was writing a book with her. Otherwise..." She shrugged again.

The twins looked a lot alike, with dark hair, light complexions, and round bodies. Pablo Arias was about six inches taller than his sister, Maria, who was around my height. Kelly had told me that he was single and a professor of mechanical engineering at the Institute of Technology in Buenos Aires. Maria was married, a housewife with a little girl.

The maître d' showed them to our table, and we all introduced ourselves. The waiter showed up immediately, and Kelly told him to give her the check.

After we ordered, Pablo said, "So, our aunt was murdered. Have they arrested Sebastian Fernandez yet?"

"Not to my knowledge," Kelly said. "I don't even think they've questioned him."

"Why not?" Pablo's voice rose enough that it earned glances from people at the tables around us. Maria noticed and lay a hand on his arm, giving him an entreating look.

Kelly seemed to shrink a little at his tone, so I stepped in.

"I'm not sure the police are aware of their relationship," I said. "Certainly no one here at the college did until Kelly discovered it in Alice's papers."

"Señor Ortiz has apprised the authorities here," Pablo said.

"You've spoken to Señor Ortiz?" I asked.

"Of course. Several times. He isn't impressed with the local police."

Maria asked him something in Spanish, and he replied in the same language. I got the impression that her English wasn't very good. Pablo, though, spoke with very little accent.

"I'll be speaking to the police tomorrow," he said. "Maria doesn't feel safe. Who knows what that man will do."

We ate our meal, with Kelly telling them about the college and the surrounding area. Pablo often translated for his sister. But anytime the conversation veered toward Alice and her death, Pablo got agitated, and his voice rose.

I prayed that Dr. Fernandez didn't show up for dinner. He didn't, and we managed to finish eating and pack the twins into a taxi and off to their hotel.

"Well, they have an interesting relationship with their stepfather, don't they?" Kelly said as we watched the taxi drive away.

"Yes, I wouldn't want to be standing between Pablo and Sebastian if they ever run into each other. Have you spoken to Señor Ortiz lately?"

She nodded. "A couple of days ago. He doesn't understand why Kagan didn't rush out and arrest Fernandez as soon as Ortiz informed him of Fernandez and Alice's history."

"A little thing like evidence? Proof?"

Kelly shrugged. "That was the problem Ortiz ran into in Argentina when Alice's sister died. From what I can dig up, a lot of people suspected Fernandez, including the major newspapers in Buenos Aires. But no evidence. No witnesses. Lots of motive, though. Fernandez and his lawyer buddy walked away rich."

"But that was a long time ago, and he did walk away. All the negative publicity doesn't seem to have hurt him too bad," I said. "Why kill Alice now?"

"It hurt him enough that he left Argentina to get away from it. You know how small and insular Wicklow is. How would you like to have people whispering behind your back every time you walked into the Faculty Club?"

I could understand that. I'd only been there a couple of months, and I already had a reputation as a busybody because I'd helped to solve a string of murders. What I didn't understand was how people could just go about their daily lives and ignore the fact that a killer walked among them. Didn't that scare them? And if Alice's death wasn't cause for alarm, Colby's death certainly was.

※

Kelly had volunteered to play tour guide for the Arias twins. She loved doing that, and one of her hobbies was the history of Wicklow College, the town of Wicklow, and the area of Pennsylvania around them.

The tour had to wait, though, until after Pablo visited Lieutenant Kagan at the police department. Then he met with Señor Ortiz at the Wayfarer.

While we waited for him, we took Maria for a walking tour of the town, which included a visit to Lowell Carragher's bookstore. He spoke to her in Argentinian Spanish, charming her as he did all the women he interacted with, and showed her a couple of shelves in the back of his shop that held Spanish-language books. For the first time since I met her, I saw her smile, and her personality blossomed. I discovered that she did speak some English—better than my Spanish.

That didn't last long, however. When we finally met with her brother, she retreated into her shell.

Pablo greeted us with an angry rant against the police and Sam Kagan in particular. He finished by saying, "I shall speak with the embassy, and a friend in Buenos Aires has offered to help."

I kept my mouth shut, and Kelly kind of rolled her eyes a little when she faced away from him. Having traveled extensively in other countries, I knew how little a foreign embassy could do, and since Alice was an American citizen, I doubted they would even respond to him.

By the time I got home, I was frazzled. Being around Pablo was like walking on eggshells, never sure what might set him off. And I could tell that while Kelly was being nice and trying to accommodate the twins, she was worried about her own situation. Her offer to help Alice with her memoir had turned into a far more perilous adventure than she'd ever imagined.

My landline phone rang. It scared the hell out of me, because that had never happened before. At first, I couldn't figure out what was making the noise. I approached it like an unknown animal, and carefully picked up the handset.

"Hello?"

"Dr. Robinson?"

"Yes?"

"This is Shirley Thompson from the Post-Gazette. I was wondering if you might have some time to meet with me."

"What is this in regard to?" I vaguely knew that was the major newspaper in Pittsburgh, but I never read it.

"The death of Alice Henderson. I understand she was your next-door neighbor at Wicklow College."

Oh, Lord. As the daughter of a man on the Witches' Council, I had been schooled from an early age to avoid the press like plague carriers.

"I'm afraid I didn't know her well, and I have nothing to add beyond what the police have released to the public," I said. "Good day, Ms. Thompson."

"But—"

CHAPTER 11

One thing about journalists is they are far more persistent than cops. If Kagan had pursued his suspects with the zeal Shirley Thompson pursued her story, we would all have been safer.

The following morning, when I left my apartment to go to my office, Thompson was waiting for me. Her ambush had about the same subtlety as the CIA officer's.

"Dr. Robinson! Just a moment of your time!"

I turned to see a young woman hurrying toward me. I knew she wasn't a student due to the way she was dressed, but she wasn't wearing the dark business-suit look of one of my investigative tormentors.

"Shirley Thompson," she announced as she stopped in front of me. Light brown hair pulled back into a short ponytail, green open-collared shirt under a buff blazer, and a yellow pencil skirt with a top-of-the-knee hemline. Flats. A large bag slung over her shoulder, and she held a small microphone with a wire leading back into the bag.

"I told you on the phone that I don't know anything," I said.

"Is it true that Kelly Grace is writing a book about Alice Henderson?"

"You should talk to Ms. Grace."

"She's not talking. You do know that she's been arrested for the murder of a government agent, don't you?"

"I have nothing to say, Ms. Thompson. This is private property, and if you continue to harass me, I'll call the campus police."

At that point, it occurred to me that she was already inside the College's wards, so she had at least a small bit of magic. I put out my hand and grabbed her microphone. Surprise—maybe, *shock* would be a better word—bloomed on her face. I dropped the microphone and stepped on it. The crunching noise was rather satisfying.

Leaning close, I said, "You know better than this. Do you really think that sensationalizing murder at a college of the arcane is a good idea? Your bosses may think a story about this mess will sell papers, but I can guarantee the Witches' Council will not be amused. Good day, Ms. Thompson."

I left her standing there with an astonished look on her face. As soon as I was out of her sight, I pulled out my phone and called the chief of the campus police.

"Alistair? Savanna Robinson. There's a reporter from the Pittsburgh paper on campus, sticking a microphone in people's faces. Her name is Shirley Thompson."

"Oh, Lord," Alistair said. "That's all I need. Thanks."

As I passed the spot where I had been accosted by the grabby CIA guy, I realized that he had been even farther on campus. I decided that I needed to be careful, or I'd be joining Kelly in jail.

Or maybe I could play matchmaker, and sic Thompson on one of the CIA guys.

After my morning classes, I went to the Faculty Club for

lunch. I walked through the door and saw Kelly being seated, so I joined her.

"There's a reporter from the Post-Gazette roaming around," she muttered as she studied the specials.

"Yes, she phoned, and then ambushed me when I left the house this morning. How much magic does someone have to have to bypass the wards around this place?"

She looked a little surprised. "I'm not sure. I suppose it could be latent."

"Wonderful. So she might not even know she's a witch?"

"Possible. Why?"

"Because I said something stupid. She irritated me, and I warned her not to get crosswise of the Witches' Council."

"Well, we can look her up. I have access to the Council's registry, and if she's registered, she'll show up there."

I nodded. "Yeah, I have access to that, too. I looked up Colby and found that he wasn't in the Council's good graces."

"It must be tough when everybody hates you. I mean, I'm sorry he's dead, and I was horrified to find him in my yard, but it wasn't like being sorry the way I'd have been if it was the postman or someone I didn't know."

I chuckled. "He had a way of making himself distasteful."

Sebastian Fernandez came to the door and was escorted to a table near us.

Kelly leaned close and said, "I've never seen him with anyone else."

"No friends on the faculty?"

She shook her head. "Not that I know of."

"I wonder if Kagan or the CIA are even aware of him. Maybe I'll drop a word to Kathleen Furman," I said.

All through our meal, Fernandez kept glancing at us, and we kept glancing at him. It was almost funny.

I had some time that afternoon, so I accessed the Council registry to search for Sebastian Fernandez. I was astounded with what showed up on my screen. Whereas Colby's profile was two pages long, there was a novella about Fernandez.

It included the whole scandal surrounding his wife's death and his subsequent appropriation of the vineyard. The Council's investigators were as convinced as Tomas Ortiz that Fernandez had killed his wife and forged the will that made him rich. But that wasn't the major crime he was implicated with.

His brother had been an admiral in the Argentine navy, and one of the plotters who overthrew the democratic government in the mid-1970s. The so-called 'dirty war' over the next decade had involved the false imprisonment, torture, and deaths of more than thirty thousand of the military regime's enemies.

Fernandez's move to Wicklow seemed to be more related to his association with the brutal junta than his notoriety due to his wife's death. And the Council had evidence that a large donation to the College had bought his teaching position. I wondered how much of that Kathleen Furman knew.

Alice was in Argentina during that time, which also included the Falklands War with Britain. The Argentine coup and subsequent military junta were supported by the CIA, along with operations in Chile, Paraguay, Uruguay, and Brazil under the umbrella of something called Operation Condor. It was evidently designed to rid South America of communists and socialists. Which meant that if Fernandez was involved, then his escape to Pennsylvania might have been at least partially facilitated by the CIA. That shined a whole new light on why the Agency was so interested in Wicklow.

CHAPTER 12

Kelly came over after work, and I filled her in on what I'd learned. She was very quiet for a while.

"You know, some of Alice's papers refer to Operation Condor," she finally said. "I vaguely had heard of it, but that all started before I was born. I'll bet my dad would know more about it."

"According to what I read this afternoon, the military junta collapsed in part due to the Falklands war with England," I said. "I'm sure there were some interesting discussions in Washington between the CIA and MI-6 over that. I doubt the CIA planned for their puppets in Argentina to attack one of our allies. And the military government facilitated death squads to disappear their enemies."

Kelly shook her head. "If Alice and Fernandez were involved in any of that, it explains why the CIA is here. You know they don't want anyone dredging up any such covert operation that went that far off the rails."

"Your book. That's why everyone is so concerned about it. Did I tell you that Fernandez approached me? He wanted to warn me off from Tomas Ortiz. Said he was deranged."

"Well, I'm sure Fernandez is concerned about multiple issues. If he did buy his way into Wicklow, I might expect a visit from Dr. Phillips."

"Who wasn't even here at the time, let alone in charge?" I was skeptical. "Isn't there a board who directs the College's affairs? Some people on that who have CIA connections, maybe?"

I was surprised at her answer.

"Actually, no. Wicklow—including its investment fund—is overseen by the tenured faculty. Edmund was voted to college president by the faculty. If you last long enough, you'll join the club. There is, of course, a representative from the Witches' Council."

"And that is?"

"She's a professor and department chair in Elemental Magic, so she's a member of the Faculty Council anyway. You might have seen her with David. Older woman, white hair, always wears a colorful crocheted shawl, no matter what else she's wearing. She's getting near retirement age."

I vaguely remembered seeing her on campus.

"So, is it the Faculty Council who approves hiring and contracts?" I asked.

She shrugged. "They rubber-stamp them. Carver does all the hiring of faculty, and as long as he fulfills Human Resources' requirements, they don't care. Dr. Phillips reviews them, of course, and usually the department chair proposes the candidate to Carver. It would take the Faculty Council paying attention to actually question a proposed candidate."

"Does that mean my hiring was all due to Jerome Carver?"

Kelly laughed. "They were probably so relieved he found someone that they didn't even look at your credentials."

For the first time, I understood how insular Wicklow was. The school was incestuous, a law unto itself in some ways.

THE REVENGE GAME

There was no outside oversight of anything, not even its finances.

※

Leaving my apartment the following morning, I saw the CIA creep who had assaulted me walking through the breezeway ahead of me. I followed him through Howard Quad and into Scholar's Quad, where he turned into the Administration Building.

After climbing the steps and entering the building, I saw him walk down the hall to my right. At the end of the hall, he knocked on a door and entered. I was curious who he was going to see, and walked down that way.

The name on the door was Dr. Sebastian Fernandez. I found a place to sit on the nearby staircase, and waited. Twenty minutes later, CIA guy came out and walked back down the hall, then exited the building.

I climbed the stairs to the second floor. As I opened my office door, I realized that Fernandez's office was directly below mine. I had warded my door and windows, but hadn't thought to make the office soundproof. I put the books and my briefcase on my desk, and cast a spell to correct that oversight.

While I was doing that, in the back of my mind, I replayed the scene I had just witnessed. There was no longer a question as to whether Fernandez had a connection to the CIA. A thought struck me, and I turned on my computer. I was supposedly in the office for students to come in, but early in the term, they rarely did. As final exams approached, I would see a lot of them—some possibly for the first time—desperately seeking a magical solution to a lack of studying all trimester.

It turned out that Argentina had conducted some prosecutions of the military junta and the independent right-wing death squads. They hadn't expended much effort to find the criminals who fled the country, and the United States had turned a blind eye to the entire affair. The State Department had released a lot of documents concerning Operation Condor—an operation carried out by a previous administration—and then ignored it as something only of interest to historians.

But with enough digging, I found that Sebastian Fernandez was considered a wanted man in Argentina, and the government had revoked his passport. He became a U.S. citizen shortly after coming to Wicklow. Normally, it would take at least five years of residency in the country, but Fernandez had somehow jumped to the front of the line.

I already knew his brother was a member of the ruling military junta, but Sebastian was suspected of organizing some of the death squads. No wonder he found Wicklow so comfortable.

I relayed all that to Kelly when I met her for lunch, along with some printouts—such as Fernandez's arrest warrant.

"Well, this is certainly juicy enough to put in the book," Kelly said.

"Who was the president of Wicklow at the time?" I asked.

"Ah," she said, and then stared off into space for a couple of minutes. "That is a can of worms, isn't it? And what was the payoff? A donation to the Wicklow Foundation, or a bribe to an individual?"

She settled herself in her chair, then said, "Thirty-five years ago? Manuel Blanco. He was Spanish and his family was associated with the dictator Franco. He was only president for five or six years. Died of a heart attack."

"How large was that footprint the police found in your flowerbed?" I asked.

"Large. Like a size eighteen, or something absurd. By the way, the cops are dropping the charges against me. Myron wants me to sue them. I'm hoping the threat will make them return all my documents."

CHAPTER 13

I invited David over for dinner. He showed up with a wonderful bottle of wine. Unfortunately, it was far better than the bottle I used to cook the *coq au vin*. Oh, well.

In San Francisco, I always made the French chicken stew in a slow cooker, but the dearth of electrical outlets in my kitchen forced me to cook the dish the old-fashioned way. As a result, it wasn't quite ready when he came, so I set a small cheese tray on the coffee table in the living room while he uncorked the wine.

"I don't have a decanter," I told him.

"I'm not that much of a wine snob," he responded. "Lowell is more persnickety." He grinned. "I got this on sale."

He poured the wine, and I sat down and snagged a slice of cheese.

"Kelly told me at lunch that the cops are dropping the charges."

David raised an eyebrow. "Oh, really? That's good news. Myron is semi-retired. He was a big-time criminal lawyer in Philadelphia, made his money, and moved back here to a quieter life."

"How do you know him?"

"He was one of my roommates here as an undergrad."

We chatted a bit, then the timer went off in the kitchen, and I served dinner. I didn't have a real dining table, just a small one in the kitchen that I used most of the time, and my desk in the main room that I used when having guests.

After dinner, as we contemplated each other over the last of the wine, I said, "I discovered that some parts of the faculty website are off-limits to me because I'm not tenured yet."

A wry smile twisted his mouth. "Good ol' stuffy Wicklow. Can't have the transients mucking about in our business."

"But you have access to all of it, don't you?"

"Yes. Almost all of it. HR stuff is off-limits for the most part. Why?"

I told him what I'd learned about Sebastian Fernandez, and his relationship with Alice.

He thought about it, sipping his wine. I finished mine, got up, and brought a pair of snifters and a bottle of cognac from the kitchen, and poured us each a dram.

"Okay. What is it that you want to know that you think I might be able to provide?" he asked.

"I don't have access to files restricted to the Faculty Council."

He chuckled. "Ah. And you think that a fine dinner and good company will loosen my ethics. Perceptive woman." He took a sip of his drink. "What exactly are you looking for?"

"Anything pertaining to the hiring of Sebastian Fernandez thirty-five years ago."

David frowned. "A very bad enemy."

"He did his best to impress me with that fact."

"This is about Alice?"

"Yes, she was his sister-in-law. She came here following him, and she believed that he killed her half-sister. I found evidence that there is a warrant for his arrest in Argentina for his role in the Dirty War in the seventies and early eighties."

He shrugged. "I can try. You know that was before everything was computerized. Any documents might or might not have been scanned. You might also see if Lowell still has any contacts in Argentina."

"How about financial information? I'm trying to figure out if he bought his position."

"Hmmm. I would think any large donation would be recorded in the Council minutes. Those I know were scanned, all the way back to the beginning."

"What if the donation was a personal one to the president?"

David shook his head. "I wouldn't necessarily dismiss that. Nothing illegal about it, since we're not a public institution. You'd have to get Manuel Blanco's tax returns, or maybe his bank statements. Good luck with that."

He was quiet for a little while, taking an occasional sip of his drink.

"The proposal for his appointment will be in the Council minutes," he said. "Let's start with that."

"How was my appointment greeted?" I asked.

"With relief. Most of us thought that finding someone to fill two positions was a pipe dream." He smiled. "You're a unicorn, Dr. Robinson."

He finished his drink and stood to go. I walked him to the door, where he turned to me.

"Thank you for a lovely dinner. I'll take a look through the records and see what I can find."

For a moment, I thought he might bend down and kiss me. He stared at my face for a long moment, then turned back to the door and let himself out.

It appeared that I was going to have to make the first move if I wanted more from our friendship. The problem was, I hadn't decided if I did, but he was tempting.

I was getting ready to go to work the following morning when my landline rang. I eyed it with skepticism but picked up anyway.

"Hello?"

"Dr. Robinson?" A woman's voice.

"Yes?"

"This is Kathleen Furman. Is there a time we can meet? I have some questions about the current situation in Wicklow."

I sighed, and tried to decide what to do about her. I had a distaste for allowing investigators into my apartment.

"Perhaps we could have dinner tonight," I said. "There's a little bistro just off Main Street on Fifth. Make a reservation for six o'clock."

"That would be perfect. Thank you."

I hung up, already planning to stick her with the bill. I figured her expense account could afford it. While Ortiz and the Arias twins were staying at the College's favored hotel, the Wayfarer, Furman and the CIA were booked into the Grand, the fanciest place in town. Although if it were up to me, I'd stay out at Carragher's Retreat. A little more rustic, but a far better restaurant, and no college-student bar next door.

I wasn't in the mood to meet with Furman, but I knew that if I stonewalled her, she'd complain to Santa Fe that I wasn't being cooperative. The next call I'd get after that would be from my father. But maybe it could work to my advantage. She might know more about Sebastian Fernandez than I'd been able to glean from the Witches' Council records.

And I'd far rather talk to a Council investigator than the smug jerks from the CIA.

CHAPTER 14

The restaurant I suggested to Kathleen Furman was the closest thing Wicklow had for French cuisine. The menu had several country-French dishes, a selection of crêpes, a couple of German and Italian items, and small-bistro décor that vaguely looked French to someone who had never seen the real thing. Both Kelly and Lowell liked the place, and Lowell's bookstore was only a block away.

She was already seated when I arrived. I took my seat and a menu from the maître d' and ordered a bottle of *Chateau neuf du Pape*. Furman looked mildly uncomfortable, and I wondered if she expected me to stick her with the bill. Maybe she was a bit clairvoyant, or psychic. Those would be useful for a Witches' Council investigator. For my entrée, I decided on the lamb chops with a cognac Dijon cream sauce, and hoped the chef knew how to make it properly.

I had no intention of letting her control the conversation. Before she had a chance to say anything, I said, "Tell me about Sebastian Fernandez."

"Uh, the professor at the College?"

"The leader of Argentine death squads."

That flustered her. She didn't know what to say, or what to do with her hands.

"I know that the CIA has some kind of interest in him," I continued. "I saw one of their agents meet with him in his office."

The waiter showed up to take our orders. When he left us alone again, I leaned across the table.

"I believe you were brought here to evaluate the death of Jefferson Colby. What did you determine?"

She shook her head. Her interrogation of me had turned on its head, and Agent Furman wasn't very nimble. I almost felt sorry for her, but instead I stared at her, silently demanding an answer.

"Uh, he died of a heart attack, a myocardial infarction. There, uh, there wasn't anything I could detect as to its cause."

I nodded. "You have the healer's gift?"

"Uh, somewhat."

Leaning back in my chair, I regarded her, then said, "What, exactly, did the Council send you here to do? Obviously, Agent Colby's demise wasn't at the top of their agenda. Was it Alice's murder?"

She sighed, then said, "Your father was my graduate advisor. He always asked questions I dreaded. I'm glad I don't have to take any classes from you."

I burst out laughing, and other people in the restaurant turned to look at us.

"You're here to monitor the CIA," I said. "Well, I hope your superiors gave you some of the history. But I'll tell you now that everyone is interested in finding every scrap of paper Alice Henderson ever had, but no one seems to be interested in catching her killer. That is the scandal, Ms. Furman. Now, tell me about Sebastian Fernandez."

I could see she was struggling with herself, but finally she said, "The, uh, the Council is worried about the CIA's involvement here. At least some of the Council's members consider the Supernatural Investigations Unit as a rogue organization. A dangerous organization. Yes, we know about Dr. Fernandez, but the CIA provides cover for him. Has done so since he was in Argentina."

"Did their agents help him to escape responsibility for his wife's death?"

She nodded. "They sheltered him. We suspect they helped him gain control of her estate."

"Because he knew they were promoting and sheltering the death squads?"

"Probably. He was staunchly anti-Communist, and that's all they cared about."

Our meal came, and I enjoyed it immensely. Furman picked at her food. When we finished and our plates were cleared, I decided to help her out a little.

"You said you had questions for me about the CIA presence?"

She perked up a bit. "Yes. I was wondering what contacts you've had with them."

I told her about Colby, Porter—the guy who attempted to get physical with me—the men who came to my place looking for Kelly, and the agent I saw going into Fernandez's office.

"That's pretty much it, except for the men following me around." I motioned to the front of the restaurant, where a man could be seen across the street, leaning against the doorway of a closed shop. "It's not always the same guy. But any time I go out, I have company."

"Are they always so obvious?"

"Yes. I think they do it for intimidation. I doubt they think I'm going to lead them to a secret stash of Alice's papers."

She didn't ask me anything else, so I asked her, "Do you think the CIA helped Fernandez to get his appointment at Wicklow?" A thought struck me. "Or did the CIA have the help of someone on the Witches' Council to get that appointment?"

I wanted to play poker with that woman so badly. The stricken look on her face when I asked the question was all the confirmation I needed.

"Is that why you're here? To cover up any embarrassment to the Witches' Council? Someone is afraid the CIA will throw the Council under the bus?"

She stared at me like a bird facing a snake. I had what I needed, so I collected my purse and pushed my chair back.

"I strongly suggest you tell your handler this is a bad idea. Time to retire. Do not play ball with the spooks. And tell them I will take any actions against Kelly Grace personally. Thank you for dinner."

I walked out, thinking that I should be very careful going home. I had arrived by bus, but that might not be the best idea if Furman found enough courage—or cowardice—to inform anyone what I suspected.

I pulled my phone from my purse and called Steven.

"Got your pants on?" I asked when he answered.

"Yes, why?"

"I need a ride home. Asap. I'm at The Sports Center." That was a bar only half a block away. Not my normal kind of place, but one sure to have a lot of customers due to its twenty TV sets.

"On my way. Should I bring my wand?"

"It might not be a bad idea."

"Give me five minutes."

I hung up, walked into the bar, and ordered a white wine.

I sat at the bar, in a place I could see both the front and back doors. No one wearing a suit followed me into the place. I chuckled to myself. If they had, they would stick out. In a bar full of men watching reruns of football games, not a single one wore a suit.

Steven walked in about ten minutes later.

"Sorry. Who knew parking could be a problem in Wicklow? This place is popular."

"Did you see anyone hanging around outside?"

"Other than someone loitering around, trying to appear innocuous in a tailor-made suit? No. Why?"

"Only one?"

He nodded. "Do you want to hang out and see the rest of the game, or shall we go?"

"I think the game was played last Sunday, and the home team won."

His car was parked almost a block away. The man in the suit followed us.

"Not very good at this, is he?" Steven remarked.

"I don't think his normal job is as a field agent. I'm actually starting to wonder if incompetence is a job requirement for the CIA's Supernatural Investigations Unit. You know, you have magic, but you can't make it as a witch, and your grades in accounting are too low to land a job as a bookkeeper."

My companion laughed.

When we reached his two-seat sports car, we discovered he had a flat. Actually, two flats.

"That's rather distressing," I said.

"Bastards."

I pulled out my phone and called for a tow truck. "I'll pay the charges," I told Steven. "When the wrecker gets here, we'll ride with him back to the college."

I leaned against the car and waved to the lurker who was watching us from the shadow of a porch across the street.

It was two hours earlier in Santa Fe, so I had no compunction against calling my father when I got home.

"And to what do I owe this auditory visit?" he asked when he picked up the phone.

"I missed you."

"Uh-huh. And if this was twenty years ago, my next question would be, how much?"

"Oh, come on. I called when I didn't need money."

He chuckled. "A couple of times. So?"

"I understand that you know a woman named Kathleen Furman."

He took a deep breath. "Former student. How did you run into her?"

"She's here in Wicklow. Council investigator overseeing the Alice Henderson mess. Or so she's led me to believe."

After almost a minute of silence, he said, "This may be more complicated than I thought. Let me check on a few things. It may take a couple of days, but I'll call you."

"Okay. Good night."

I stood there in my kitchen, staring at the phone in my hand, and trying to figure out exactly what was going on. That reaction from my father was thoroughly unexpected.

CHAPTER 15

When I met Kelly the following day for lunch at the Faculty Club, she appeared to be a bit flustered. She sat down and said, "Have you ordered yet?"

I shook my head.

"You don't have any classes this afternoon, do you?" she asked.

Again, I shook my head. "I was going to do some prep work for a tutorial later this week, but it's not urgent."

"Let's get out of here. I want to go someplace quiet, and preferably remote, and get thoroughly hammered."

I grabbed my purse and stood. We walked out the backdoor of the restaurant and across the street to the parking lot near the library.

"You can drive, right?" she asked.

With a chuckle, I said, "Yes. I know how to drive. I just haven't had the money to afford a car the past few years."

We drove through town and out into the country.

"Carragher's?" I asked.

"Mm-hmm. I had two of those damned CIA goons walk in my office this morning, and they refused to leave. Even worse, they wouldn't let me leave. My only options were to sit there while they interrogated me, or assault them. And believe me, I was tempted."

After a couple of minutes, she asked, "Do you think they're fanatical enough to kill one of their own?"

I choked back a laugh. "You mean, could they have killed Colby?"

"Yeah."

"No idea. But if he died someplace else, I wouldn't put it past them to dump the body in your yard. I have no idea who might want Colby dead. I think he was in the wrong place at the wrong time—whether that was your house or someplace else."

At Carragher's, Kelly ordered a double scotch on the rocks as soon as we were handed menus. I ordered a cheese board and charcuterie, figuring it would be a quick and easy way to put something solid in her stomach. For myself, I ordered black tea. It was obvious that I was going to be driving back to town.

"Savanna, have you ever wanted to kill someone? I mean, truly contemplated actually doing it? That jerk Keith Porter came about this close to meeting his maker this morning."

"I have killed someone, but it was in self-defense," I said. "As far as doing it because some asshole irritated me beyond all reason, I came close with a couple of those idiots from London who were looking for that stupid grimoire. The problem with striking out in anger is you might use the most effective spell, but it would be better using one less detectable."

Kelly nodded and popped a slice of cheese in her mouth, then took a large swallow of her drink. "Like that heart-stopping spell someone used on Colby. I'm not any good with that kind of magic."

"Which one is Porter? The big guy?" I asked. I hadn't sorted out all of the government agents wandering around and acting like big shots.

"Tall, incredibly handsome, with hair out of Hollywood. He's a total dick. Never met a woman who could resist him. And I think sex is the only use he has for women."

"Ah. Yeah, he's the one I saw go into Fernandez's office, and also the one who accosted me in the breezeway in front of my apartment."

"Well, he was attempting to browbeat me into giving up and turning all of mine and Alice's documents over to him—including the chapters of the book I've already written."

"He didn't happen to leave anything personal behind, did he? You know, a strand of hair? Blood from a paper cut?"

She laughed. "If there was blood, it would have been from something a lot worse than a paper cut. Letter opener at the very least."

Kelly signaled the waiter and ordered another scotch when he came over. I took the opportunity to order a pot pie for myself, and fish and chips for my friend.

"I was thinking we could craft an exclusion ward for him," I said when the waiter left.

"I was thinking more along the lines of a trap," she responded.

"A spider's web? There are some nasty variations on that type of spell. Unfortunately, many of them cross some of the Council's lines. If I captured someone that way, I would either make it as vanilla as possible or I'd make it lethal. You don't want Mr. Gift-to-women to cry to the Council that you abused him."

That got the first smile I had seen from her that day.

"You know some unusual magic," she said.

"I'm a scholar. One of my hobbies is the magic our ancestors used when the witch hunts went crazy in the fifteenth and sixteenth centuries."

The waiter brought our food and another drink for Kelly.

"There are legends of some pretty spectacular magical displays," Kelly said.

"Yes. As far as I can tell, from extensive research, the legends surrounding the Battle of Angers are somewhat mild compared to the actual events."

She blinked at me. "You're kidding."

"There were mages who actually manipulated the weather. I've been to the battleground, and there are huge craters—you can see them even five centuries later. More than seventy thousand French, Norman, and English soldiers were killed. Less than ten thousand were counted as wounded. And Kelly, the casualties on the witches' side were a few dozen—mostly due to burn out."

Kelly took a swallow of whisky, then stared down at the contents of her glass.

"Do you think there are witches that powerful nowadays? I mean, no one teaches battle magic anymore—at least not formally. Do they?"

"I think they do in some places. Rumors out of China. Who knows what they do in Africa, but I'm sure the governments down there use magic as a weapon—both against each other and internally to control their populations."

Sub-Saharan Africa was controlled by strongmen—some witches, some not, but at the very least supported by strong witches. When Europeans first invaded Africa, they assumed the people there were weak due to a lack of technology. The backlash of magic tossed the Europeans out and showed that technology was only one way of building a civilization.

"But you've studied such magic, not just the history," she said.

"Yes." I chuckled. "And yes, I've tried some rather unusual spells in controlled environments, but I've never even contemplated testing a spell such as the triple circle used to kill ten thousand men in a single stroke at the Battle of Green Hammerton in Yorkshire."

"A triple circle?"

"Three circles of thirteen witches linked together like a shamrock. The English troops came down the road toward York, and just outside the village of Green Hammerton, the witches ambushed them. One massive strike, then they retired to the village pub for lunch."

"I just want Porter and his buddies to go away and leave me alone," Kelly said.

"I'll check my grimoires for unwanted-boyfriend spells."

CHAPTER 16

I had borrowed Kelly's car a couple of times, so I was familiar with it. I pulled out of Carragher's driveway onto the highway heading back into Wicklow. Highway was a rather ambitious term for the narrow two-lane paved road that followed the Allegheny River north out of Wicklow.

I came around a corner to find a deer—a buck with a large rack of antlers—standing in the middle of the road. My first instinct was to slam on the brakes and steer away from the animal.

Kelly screamed and then covered her head with her arms when it became apparent that I was going to hit it.

Although I pumped the brakes and slowed, I steered straight through the illusion.

"What?" Kelly uncurled, and her head whipped around to look behind us.

"Illusion." I continued toward town. "I think someone wanted us to drive into a tree."

"You have a suspicious mind," she said, then turned to look behind us again. "And I think I'm glad you do. How did you know?"

"Whoever cast it isn't very good, or very strong. It wasn't solid, and I could see through it. I could see the trees."

I thought about that as we drove into town. The thin illusion wasn't what tipped me off initially.

"It was like looking at a picture. A two-dimensional picture. The deer didn't move at all," I announced.

"Yeah, thinking back on it, I saw that as well. But I'm pretty hammered. Savanna, I can sleep on your couch."

"Nah, I'll drop you off and take the bus. Not a problem."

It was only two o'clock in the afternoon, and I could still do the prep work for those classes.

The walk from Kelly's house to the nearest bus stop was only two blocks, but during that time I saw two of the CIA men, including Keith Porter. He pulled a car in across the street shortly after we arrived. The timing was such that I suspected he had been following us. Possibly the witch who cast the deer illusion? If so, that confirmed my suspicions that they were trying to intimidate me.

The other guy was waiting near the bus stop. He sat in a car and watched me while I waited twenty minutes for the bus. Not terribly subtle.

I spent the rest of the afternoon preparing materials for students to use in the lab exercise for my apothecary class the following day. I could have had a graduate student do the work, but unfortunately, the grad students who had been assigned to me at the beginning of the trimester were either dead or in prison. I made a note to myself to arrange for some new cannon fodder for the winter term. Hopefully, the next group would fare better.

So, I was cooking a late dinner when my father called.

"Sorry it took so long to get back to you," he said when I

answered. "About your Kathleen Furman, she wasn't exactly sent there by the Council. She's there at the direction of a Councilor, Marcus LePage."

I knew the name and could vaguely picture the man.

"And?" I asked.

"You were right. He was one of the people who originally organized the Supernatural Investigations Unit for the CIA. And it appears he was instrumental in bringing Sebastian Fernandez out of Argentina and helping him land his position at Wicklow. He and a former president of the College were friends."

I thought about it.

"Thanks. I guess I feel smart that I had worked that out, but I'm not sure what good it does me."

"Well," he said, "it clarifies whose side Furman is on."

"Yes, but the Council still doesn't have an independent investigator on site. Is LePage a friend of yours?"

"Not really. What did you think of that state cop I sent down there last time? Barclay?"

"I thought he was quite sharp, but isn't his expertise in computers?"

My dad chuckled. "That's his mundane expertise. He's a very good witch and a very good cop. I'll send him along."

I wasn't going to complain. Barclay was also extremely pleasant to look at—and single.

After we hung up, I sat down and wrote a few things on my computer, printed out a sheet of paper, tucked it into an envelope, and took it into town.

Shirley Thompson was staying at the Wayfarer. I left the envelope for the reporter at the front desk, then walked back to campus. The night was rather brisk, but there wasn't any wind, and it was quiet and peaceful—just me and the stars.

As I reached campus, a car in the parking lot across the street from my apartment started, turned on its lights, and entered the street headed for town. It passed me, and I saw that Pablo Arias was driving. Tomas Ortiz sat next to him, and Pablo's sister was in the back seat. None of them seemed to pay any attention to me.

Glancing up at Alice's apartment, I didn't see any lights on. That didn't mean no one had been in there, but I didn't see what good it would do them. Damned near everything had been stripped out of the place.

Entering my own apartment, I looked around and tried to imagine where I might be able to create a hiding place. The outside walls were solid stone, the inside walls had wallpaper over plaster and wainscotting. The massive stone fireplace might offer an opportunity to create a space by pulling out one of the stones.

It was November and quite cold outside, but I had yet to try and start a fire. Baseboard hot water was supplied to all the apartments from a boiler in the basement—the same boiler that filled the enormous claw-foot tub. As far as I could figure, the heater had three settings: off, almost warm enough, and too damned hot. The first setting was what I'd used the first couple of months of residence. Around Samhain, I'd turned it on and experimented with it. I would have to ask David about the fireplace. If I did use it, I'd have to find wood.

CHAPTER 17

Three days after my conversation with my father, I answered a knock on the door to find Lieutenant James Barclay of the Pennsylvania State Police.

"Well, this is a pleasant surprise," I said with a smile. "Come in."

"Thank you. Have you seen this?" He held out a newspaper.

I scanned the front page of the Pittsburgh paper as I led him through my foyer, and below the fold, found the article he evidently thought was of interest.

Suspicious Death at Wicklow College Draws Federal Interest

The byline was Shirley Thompson. The girl had followed up on my letter. She didn't really have anything to report except rumors that Alice had worked for an intelligence agency in her youth, and that the agency was taking an interest in her death. Since by law the CIA shouldn't have been taking an interest in anything in Pennsylvania, it was newsworthy. The story included the first public acknowledgement of official interest in Alice's papers.

"That reporter is like a bad rash," I said. "Every time you try to get rid of her, she pops up again."

"Well, this story can be viewed as both good and bad," Barclay said as he took a seat in my sitting room. "The Council and the CIA won't like the exposure, but I can use it to politely suggest the spooks decamp and leave Wicklow alone."

I went into the kitchen to put the kettle on and rummage through the refrigerator for some day-old apple bread.

"She only mentions Alice's murder," I said. "You do know that one of their agents died here also, right?"

"And if he didn't come here, he might still be alive. In their world, cause and effect can get pretty murky."

I brought in the tea service and the bread, and set them down on the coffee table.

"How long are you in town?"

He shrugged. "Detached service until the mess here gets cleared up. Officially, I have office space in Chief Crumley's office." Alistair Crumley was chief of the campus police. He had authority from the Witches' Council but not from any mundane government. Barclay being there would add that level of authority.

"So," he said, taking a bite of apple bread and a sip of his tea, "tell me what you know."

"Well, the smart money is on Sebastian Fernandez. He wouldn't want Alice's memoir to paint him as a fascist and a murderer. Of course, he's had thirty years to kill her, so one might wonder what took him so long. He's a very large man, so I also have to wonder if he wears a size eighteen shoe that matches the print in Kelly Grace's garden. That's where the dead CIA agent was found. But, Lieutenant, everyone and their dogs are far more interested in Alice's papers and what she might have told Kelly than they are in solving her murder."

"Officially, Agent Colby died of a heart attack."

"Officially, Agent Colby wasn't even here, was he? Unofficially, Agent Colby was an ass who was lucky he reached the age of thirty-seven. But if you think his heart attack was unassisted, I have a bridge I'd like to sell you."

Barclay laughed. "I was told the agent in charge here is a Keith Porter."

"Who held Kelly Grace prisoner in her office while he interrogated and attempted to intimidate her for two hours earlier this week. He's lucky he hasn't tried that on me, but he did put his hands on me once. If he has a heart attack, I'll probably be a worthy suspect."

After about an hour, Barclay said, "I think I need to have a chat with Ms. Furman this afternoon. Are you free for dinner?"

"Yes. Do you like walleye?"

"Love it."

"I have just the place."

Barclay picked me up a little after five o'clock, and we drove out to Carragher's Retreat. I wasn't sure if Lowell would be out there, so I directed the lieutenant to stop by the bookstore.

"I think it's important that you meet Lowell Carragher," I said. "He seems to be the person—other than Kelly—who knows where all the bodies are buried and the skeletons are hidden in this town. He grew up here, went to college here, and knew Alice fairly well."

It seemed that every time I entered Lowell's shop he was reading a book. I supposed it was pretty boring when he didn't have any customers.

"Lowell, this is Lieutenant James Barclay of the Pennsylvania State Police and emissary of the Witches' Council. James, Lowell Carragher, local know-it-all." I gave Lowell a fond smile. "And I mean that in the most positive way."

The two men shook hands, and Lowell said, "I thought we already had a watchdog from the Council."

"Sometimes the watchdogs need watching," Barclay said. "I understand that you knew Alice Henderson quite well."

"Probably as well as anyone. I can tell you that she didn't get suddenly depressed and throw herself out a window. Alice was fond of dramatic entrances and exits, but that would be a little too uninspiring."

Barclay laughed. "I have an appointment to meet with Lieutenant Kagan tomorrow and I'll go over the case file. I've already seen the autopsy report, and it doesn't look like a suicide."

Barclay and I left and drove out to the resort on the river.

"A bookstore and a resort?" Barclay asked.

"And a mall across the river, plus a few other odds and ends. Probably about a third of the town. His sister runs the resort, and I think he's training a nephew to run the mall. I've also been told he was in Naval Intelligence, stationed in South America."

The drive out to the resort took only a few minutes. After we were seated by a window overlooking the river, I told him about the illusion of a deer in the road that Kelly and I had encountered.

"Well, that's a little more subtle than a spike strip across the road," he said.

"But possibly just as dangerous. More difficult to prove as well. The SIU boys they sent out here are more than a little pushy. They're young, and I get the feeling they have something to prove."

The waiter brought our wine and took our orders. I held up my glass in a toast, and Barclay clinked his against it.

"So, how did your chat with Ms. Furman go?" I asked.

"I'd love to play poker with her."

I burst out laughing. "So would I."

"I have a letter of introduction and an assignment signed by the Chairman of the Witches' Council," he said. "That's something she doesn't have. I let her know that I'll be telling the Wicklow Police and the Campus Police that she's not part of the investigation. I suggested that she should go back to wherever she came from. I know that Crumley isn't happy about the spooks, so I can count on his cooperation. All we have to worry about is Kagan. I need to convince him that I'm in charge, and that won't be easy."

Barclay had worked with Kagan earlier that fall. Kagan was okay, but a bit sloppy—with his magic, his police procedure, and his intellect.

I was concerned about another ambush on our trip back to town, but nothing untoward occurred. James—we had moved to a first-name basis—drove me to campus, then took himself to the Wayfarer.

CHAPTER 18

Barclay called me late the following morning and asked if I was free for lunch. We made arrangements to meet at the Faculty Club.

I expected Kelly would be there as well, so I made a point of going a little early and grabbing a table that would accommodate four. My preparations were rewarded when Kelly walked in with Stephen. They spotted me and made their way to my table.

"Eating alone?" Kelly asked.

"Lieutenant Barclay is joining me, but I was hoping you might show up as well."

They sat down, and Barclay showed up just as the waitress was taking our orders.

"How was your meeting with Kagan?" I asked.

Barclay chuckled. "I got the impression that he was uncomfortable. When I asked to see all the documents impounded from Ms. Henderson's apartment and Ms. Grace's home, I found out why. Some documents that were logged in as evidence are missing. He finally admitted that the CIA might be responsible for that."

He pulled a piece of paper from his pocket and passed it to Kelly. "Perhaps you can tell me about these."

Kelly perused the list, a deep furrow between her eyebrows and a scowl on her face.

"Bastards," she finally said. "But not a disaster. I have copies of all these." She looked up at the rest of us. "It might even be helpful. I'll have to review the documents, but this list might indicate that they are important."

"At the very least, that they are something the Agency wants to suppress," I said.

She chuckled. "What I want to know is when someone is going to enlighten Sam Kagan and the CIA about the invention of the copy machine. They seem to think if they steal a document, it's gone."

"They probably think that a blonde is too dense to use such sophisticated equipment," I said.

"Well, everything that Kagan had logged in—with the exception of this list—is now in my possession," Barclay said. "I have formal, official possession for both the State Police and the Witches' Council. Locked under an archivist's ward, witnessed by Dr. Phillips and Dr. Stone."

Kelly looked startled. "You're a librarian?"

"Yes, ma'am, I'm not just a pretty face, I'm multi-talented. And as soon as you and I go through all of that, we'll go through all the stuff that you and President Phillips have locked away, and I can put together an inventory for the Council. They are very concerned that some of Alice's documents might go missing permanently."

"Goddess, everyone wants the damned documents," I said. "Doesn't anyone care that a woman met an ugly and terrifying death?"

"Actually, I do," Barclay said. "The Council's archivists are extremely curious, however, as to why everyone wants those documents. We're operating under the assumption that they led to her death. So, we take care of that task, and move on to who managed to heave a woman who weighed a hundred and sixty pounds out that window. Kagan showed me her apartment, and I can't understand how anyone entertained the possibility of suicide."

After lunch, he said to Kelly, "Can you arrange a meeting with the Arias heirs this evening?"

"How good is your Spanish?" I asked. "Pablo is fairly fluent in English, but I'm a little concerned that anything Maria might say is usually filtered through her brother. I'm not sure that they are always in agreement."

"You're right," Kelly said. "What would you think about bringing Lowell in as an interpreter?"

I shrugged. "I can ask him. Do you think the Arias twins will accept him?"

"I don't know. It would certainly make it easier, and she likes Lowell."

Afterward, I went to my office and called Lowell, who said he would be willing to translate.

"Or, if you want to be discrete, I can sit in the background and let you know what Alice's relatives say between themselves."

"That might be an idea, but for tonight, let's play it straight."

"Will do. Call me when you know where and what time this is going to happen."

Kelly called me a few minutes later. She had made arrangements to meet with the Arias twins and Tomas Ortiz at the Faculty Club dining room after it closed for the evening. The bar stayed open for a couple of hours after that, and she reserved one of the small private dining rooms for us to use.

"I'll call Lowell and let him know. But I'm not sure why I need to be there," I told Barclay.

"Because I trust your judgement and I want you there," he replied.

***

Since I had to be at the Faculty Club at nine o'clock, it made sense to eat there. Kelly and I used our privileges to invite Lowell and Barclay as our guests.

Fernandez showed up and ignored us, while we did our best to ignore him. Thankfully, he was gone long before Ortiz and the twins arrived. By the time they did, we had moved to the back room and waited for them there.

Once everyone was in the room, Barclay closed the door and turned to me.

"Please cast a spell to block out any eavesdroppers, Savanna."

It surprised me, in part because I hadn't thought of it. I also wondered why he chose me. I was probably the most capable of a spell that blocked both electronic and magical busybodies, but how did he know that? Perhaps my father was telling Lieutenant Barclay more than I thought.

I went to the four corners of the room and drew a rune, then drew one on each side of the door to the kitchen and the door to the main dining room. Chanting an incantation, I pulled the room into its own little world. Not only was it all sound-blocked but it also would take a master mage to open either door.

I nodded to Barclay.

"Okay," he said, in the kind of voice I would use to lecture undergraduates. "We have a problem here."

I noted that Lowell, sitting next to Maria, was translating to her everything that was said.

Barclay continued. "Alice Henderson is dead, and everyone is convinced that either Sebastian Fernandez or the Central

Intelligence Agency is responsible. And everyone seems to agree that the reason that she was killed is because she planned to expose them in the book that Kelly Grace is writing. Have I captured the gist of the matter?"

He looked around, but no one contradicted him. Indeed, he had everyone's attention.

"So," Barclay said, "no one has thought of any different suspects. Such as people connected with the Argentine death squads. Or the people on the Witches' Council who bailed Fernandez out of that country and gave him his bolt hole here. Or anyone in Germany who might be concerned about their relationship with the Stasi, the East German secret police." He paused and looked around. "Ah, yes. Alice might have known some people in Communist East Germany who have prominent roles in society and government that's there now."

Kelly spoke up. "CIA doesn't seem to be worried about anything but Argentina."

"True," Barclay said. "Have you considered that people in Germany might have the same type of concerns, but the CIA doesn't care about those issues? The woman spent thirty years working for the Agency, both in Europe and South America."

"We know it was that bastard Sebastian!" Pablo said, lurching to his feet. "Murderer, thief, fascist!"

"And yet, for some reason, the local police have yet to question him," Barclay said, "in spite of the fact they found his fingerprints on several items in her apartment. I plan to speak with Lieutenant Kagan about that tomorrow."

I had planned to just watch and listen, but now I held up my hand.

"Several items? Not surfaces?"

Barclay nodded. "Correct. A glass, a bottle, a picture frame. But nothing on a doorknob, doorjamb, table, chair, or anything else."

He turned to Pablo and Maria. "Now, I need you to tell me

everything you can about Sebastian Fernandez. I need to know everything about your mother's death, about the will leaving the vineyard and winery to him, and everything you know about the sale of the estate and his disappearing from Argentina."

His questioning of the twins and Ortiz went on for more than two hours. Kelly recorded the whole thing, and Lowell translated it all for the Argentines. At times, I noticed that Maria and Lowell had some quiet conversation between themselves that he didn't translate.

Some of it was very interesting, such as when Barclay asked when the Argentines learned of Alice's plans to publish a book.

"She told us last spring," Pablo said, and Maria nodded. "That is also when she told us she had cancer."

"Pablo told me in May," Ortiz said. "I spoke with Alice in June. She wanted to get some of my case notes from my investigation into Camila's death."

We also discovered that Shirley Thompson had interviewed Ortiz earlier that day and asked to meet with Pablo. Barclay strongly urged him not to.

By the time we walked out of there near midnight, I was exhausted, and I wasn't even involved in most of it.

CHAPTER 19

My plans for Saturday included a bike ride out to Carragher's Retreat, but the skies threatened rain at the least. The temperature suggested a possibility of the first snow of the season. And although I loved my bicycle, I had serious doubts about her abilities in snow and ice. Not to mention mine.

I had grown up in Santa Fe, which sits at the base of the Sangre de Cristo mountains at a fairly high altitude. Snow in the winter was common, and a ski area was only seventeen miles away. But I had never been one for cold weather and spent most of my adult life on the West Coast. San Francisco and snow were rarely mentioned in the same paragraph. And snow wasn't something I had really considered when I was offered the job at Wicklow.

I called Kelly and asked about her plans for the weekend.

"Nothing today," she answered. "Lieutenant Barclay and I are going to spend tomorrow cataloging Alice's papers and digitizing everything for the archives in Santa Fe. Why? Do you have something in mind?"

"I was going to ride out to Carragher's, but the weather

doesn't look promising. Want to drive me? I'll buy lunch and we can talk about last night."

"Sounds like a winner. Can we stop by Lowell's on the way? I'd like to get his impressions."

Kelly picked me up and we swung by the bookstore. Lowell was helping a woman with two little boys pick out books, so we waited about twenty minutes until they were through.

"What were you and Maria chatting about last night?" I asked when we were alone.

He gave us a smile and a wink. "She says that Pablo is always easy to rile up, especially when the subject is Sebastian."

"They couldn't have been very old when their mother died," I said.

Lowell and Kelly both shook their heads.

"They were raised by their aunts," Kelly said, "Their father's sisters. Easy to rile up? The way Señor Ortiz put it to me is that Pablo's temper wouldn't be such a problem if he wasn't so impulsive."

"Do you know what their magic is?" I asked.

"Pablo is a conjurer with some alchemy," Kelly said.

"And Maria has little magic," Lowell chimed in. "Hedge witch, kitchen witch, whatever you wish to call it. I gather that her garden is quite impressive, and she promised to cook me the best meal I've ever eaten if I visit her in Buenos Aires. You've met that kind of people. Her use of magic is effortless, and totally un-ritualistic. It just flows out of her and assists her in doing whatever she wants. She doesn't even think about it."

Kelly chuckled. "Hey, I was raised by the most famous kitchen witch in the world. You don't have to explain it to me. If her magic helps, great! But if it doesn't, she really doesn't notice and spends zero seconds worrying about it. She just continues with what she's doing. It's totally unconscious. Those are the kind of witches who got burned and had no clue as to why."

It was Lowell's turn to chuckle. "And Savanna's the kind of witch who left the smoking craters where Rome and Krakow used to be."

"You flatter me, although one of my mother's ancestors put paid to Oliver Cromwell's witch hunts in Scotland. We didn't come here to talk history, though."

"One thing Maria told me," Lowell said, "is that Sebastian was strongly suspected of using coercion on their mother in order to marry her. And Ortiz told me coercion was one of the charges considered against him for his crimes during the Dirty War."

"Lovely," I said. "Combined with life magic and large feet, I think I have my prime suspect for Agent Colby's death."

"Indeed," Lowell said.

"Want to have lunch with us out in the country?" Kelly asked.

He shook his head. Leaning forward to look out the window, he said, "Tempting, but it's looking like bookstore weather."

I laughed. "Can you explain that?"

"If you're out shopping, and the weather turns nasty, hiding in a warm, cozy bookstore for a while is very tempting. You'd be surprised how many books I sell during storms."

A woman ushered four children into the store about that time, so Kelly and I took our leave. I noted that Lowell flirted almost as shamelessly with the kids as he did with their mother.

"He's a born shopkeeper," I said as we got into her car.

"Yeah. He's grooming those kids to be lifetime book buyers."

It started lightly raining on our way out of town.

"I had almost forgotten about our encounter with the deer," Kelly said as we drove past the place where we saw the illusion.

"I think our Mr. Porter was responsible for that. Lovely man. I wish the spell was a little more tangible. I don't know of a boomerang that would have much effect with an illusion."

"You mean, turn a spell back on the caster?"

"Exactly. I doubt Porter is afraid of deer."

"Huh. Beyond anything I know how to do." Kelly changed the subject. "Anything going on with you and Lieutenant Barclay?"

"I'm trying to seduce him with sweet breads, but it hasn't worked thus far. I'll keep trying."

She laughed. "You could almost lure me in with your baking, and I don't swing that way."

"Well, I know he appreciates the female form. He likes to look, but so far, he hasn't tried to touch."

"You're too shy. After you've been in Wicklow for a while, you'll learn to take the initiative."

I considered her point. When I was younger, I had been more forward with men. Maybe the staid, conservative professorial demeanor was a turnoff. I did miss having a man in my life.

We pulled into the resort parking lot about the time the light sprinkle turned a bit heavier. I had an umbrella in my purse, and Kelly had one tucked in a pocket of the driver's side door. As we made our way toward the dining room, a blue compact car pulled into the lot.

"Crap!" Kelly said. "I wondered if someone was following us."

I didn't recognize the car, but when we reached the porch, I turned to see who might be in the blue car. Due to the driver whipping out her own umbrella, I wasn't able to see her face until she came into the restaurant. By that time, Susan had led us to a table where we could see the weather outside and turned back to see to her next guest.

"Shirley Thompson?"

"Yep. Ten to one she comes over here and acts surprised to see us," Kelly said.

"I try not to bet on sure losers. Don't stare at her and we might get lucky. Have you had the Crab Louie here?"

"Huh? Oh, no. That's on special?"

Susan led the reporter to a table, but the woman kept walking over to where Kelly and I were sitting.

"Hello! I hope I'm not interrupting anything!"

"You are," I said. "Go away before I get rude."

From the expression on her face, I might as well have slapped her. I don't think she understood how tempted I was.

"Susan!" I called. "This person seems to be lost. Perhaps you can seat her on the porch."

The rain was pounding on the porch, and the outdoor furniture hadn't seen any use since before Samhain. Susan hurried over, her face red.

"I'm so sorry. Miss, please I can't have you bothering our other guests."

"She's a reporter, Susan," I said, "and she's not on the restaurant beat."

Susan's demeanor changed. "Miss, this way," she said, her voice frosty.

Thompson took the hint and a seat across the room. The original table Susan had shown her was by a window. The new one was by the kitchen.

"Sorry," Susan said when she came back to us.

"You couldn't have known," I said. "Sorry I was such a bitch, but the woman is impervious. We have both told her to go away—"

"Repeatedly," Kelly chimed in.

"Well, we'll serve her today," Susan said, "but I'll probably set some ground rules if she wants to come back."

"What's the deal with all the crab?" Kelly asked, looking at the specials page on the menu. "Crab Louie, Crab Newburg, crabcakes?"

Susan chuckled. "Our supplier showed up with a shipment of fresh Dungeness crab, and the cook got carried away. I need to sell it before it goes bad, and it would be a crime to freeze it."

"I think I can help you out," I said.

I ordered the crab salad, Kelly ordered the crab cakes, and we split a dessert. We took our time, and it was entertaining to watch Thompson checking her watch, checking her phone, and staring daggers at us since she finished her meal long before we ordered dessert.

The rain outside lessened, then turned to flakes.

"Time to get out of here," Kelly said, and I didn't argue. We paid our tab and headed to the door. Thompson got up to follow us, but Susan intercepted her. She was still talking to the reporter when Kelly wheeled her car out of the parking lot.

It was warm enough that the snow hitting the road melted immediately, but the fields by the side of the highway started turning white when we were on our way back to town.

I called Susan after Kelly let me off at my apartment.

"Susan, I want to apologize for tonight."

She laughed. "No reason for you to apologize. I did tell that reporter that she was welcome only if she didn't bother my other guests. Wicklow has never had a newspaper, and there are only a few places in town where you can buy one from Pittsburgh, or Philadelphia, or New York. Lowell sells a few. But we value our privacy."

CHAPTER 20

The world was white when I woke up. There wasn't a window in my bedroom, but when I emerged into the sitting room, I was almost blinded. The wall of windows overlooking the garden showed why the curtains I rarely closed were there.

It was barely November. Shouldn't it still be autumn? I noticed that a lot of the trees, with their colorful leaves, had branches bent from the snow.

The temperature was also cooler than I was used to. I checked the thermostat and turned it up. The building might have been a century and a half old, but the original builders built it for winter. The boilers in the basement efficiently delivered hot water to all three floors. Hot water ran through pipes in both my floor and ceiling.

I peeked out my front door and found that the maintenance crew had already cleared the portico and steps leading to the parking lot. And someone—I didn't know if it was the College or the government—had cleared the streets I could see. It didn't appear that the city or the College were slowed down at all by the three inches of snow we had overnight. San Francisco would have been paralyzed. In Santa Fe, all the kids would have been checking the ski report.

The phone rang while I was fixing breakfast.

"Sam Kagan just arrested Sebastian Fernandez," Barclay said as soon as I picked up.

"That's interesting," I said. "Sam doesn't have a reputation for arresting people unless they're innocent. What new evidence moved him to take such drastic action?"

Barclay chuckled. "He wasn't arrested for the murder of Alice Henderson. It was for the assault on Kathleen Furman."

"What?"

"Evidently the two of them had dinner together last night. They left the restaurant together, and she was found barely alive in the riverside park around nine-thirty last night by a couple of kids."

"And Kagan had what evidence to arrest Fernandez?"

"Just what I told you. Any other evidence at the scene was covered by snow. The crew at the restaurant said they didn't argue or anything."

"I had dinner with her recently. I guess I got lucky."

"There's more," Barclay said. "Someone went through Furman's hotel room. No computer, no briefcase, no paper at all. Her suitcase and toiletries are the only things left."

"Well, I think we can assume whoever attacked her took the key. Was her purse with her when they found her? How badly was she hurt?"

"They found her purse, including her wallet, but no hotel key," he said. "There's a bruise on her forehead, so I'd say there was a remote possibility she fell."

"Right. I ordered a very nice wine when I dined with her, and she barely took a sip. I don't think she was much of a drinker."

"It's pretty icy out here, and she was wearing heels."

"Yeah, I always go out walking in the snow in heels. I need to make a call," I said.

"To Santa Fe?"

"Yes."

I hung up, pulled my breakfast off the stove, and glanced at the clock. I figured I should eat breakfast before I called my dad. It was only seven o'clock in Santa Fe, and on a Sunday morning, I'd prefer he got a cup of coffee before I disturbed him.

But no sooner had I finished my omelet than someone knocked at my door. I grabbed my wand before I answered. Wicklow was starting to look a little too dangerous for my tastes.

"Chief Crumley?"

"Alistair, Dr. Robinson. May I come in?"

"Sure. I'm not really dressed for receiving company. Tea or coffee?"

"Black tea, if you please." He dropped into one of the chairs in my sitting room while I went to the kitchen to put the kettle back on the stove.

"We had another incident last night," he called.

"Kathleen Furman?"

"You've heard. Sometimes I wonder why I buy radios for my officers. They'd probably hear about things quicker through the gossip network."

"But every officer would hear a different version," I said as I carried the tea into the sitting room and put the tray on the table. "Lieutenant Barclay called me about half an hour ago."

Crumley nodded and added milk to his tea. "That makes me feel a little better. At least he called me before he called you."

"Lieutenant Barclay seems to do just about everything correctly."

"Why Furman?" he asked.

I shook my head. "I can't imagine the spooks would take her

out. She wasn't a threat to them. And she was on Fernandez's side. Helping to protect him, I mean."

The police chief nodded and took a sip of his tea. "My reasoning as well. I think Sam Kagan is barking up the wrong tree."

"Not the first time. Do you think someone from outside might have had a grudge against her?"

Chief Crumley shook his head. "No way to know. Do you suppose your father…"

"I plan to call him this morning, as soon as I think he's awake. I'll ask him to keep his ears open."

"Say hello to him for me. We worked together in Europe when we were young, you know." He sighed. "I certainly hope we aren't getting involved in any Council politics."

"I am concerned about that myself. I left Santa Fe when I graduated high school, and although I love the city and area, I've never wanted to live there again. I think I was overexposed to the ugly side of witchcraft."

The chief chuckled and nodded, took another sip of his tea, then said, "I'm supposed to be off today. I think I'll go hide for the rest of the weekend."

"Sounds like a plan. I think I'm going to pretend I'm snowed in."

I called my father as soon as Crumley left.

"Good morning," Dad answered, sounding cheerful. "How are things in the great eastern wilderness?"

"White."

"Oh, I'm so sorry to hear that. I wondered why you chose a place that gets so much snow."

"I'm working on moving the college to the Bahamas, but there's a bug in the spell I can't figure out."

He laughed. "What else is going on?"

"Katherine Furman was attacked last night."

There was a long silence, then he said, "That's not good."

"My feeling as well. The woman was irritating, but I can think of a number of less drastic ways of shutting her up. The local gendarme arrested Sebastian Fernandez."

"That doesn't make sense. Why did they arrest Fernandez?"

"He was the last person seen with her. They had dinner together."

"Pretty flimsy."

"That's our local cops. Barclay called me first thing this morning. He said the crime scene was covered in snow. I guess we're lucky we only got a few inches. She could have been buried until spring."

"You watch your back."

"Thanks, Dad. I carry my wand everywhere. I'm more afraid of getting arrested. The local cops have an uneven track record. Alistair Crumley sends his regards. He's concerned that Council politics might be spilling into Wicklow."

"I'll let you know if I hear anything."

CHAPTER 21

Call it perverse, but as much as I hated winter, I had an urge to get out into the first snow of the season. I dressed in layers—and looked a little like an arctic explorer—then caught the bus into town. One thing I hadn't considered before was a weather covering for my bicycle, so that went on my shopping list along with eggs and milk.

Barclay hadn't told me exactly where they found Kathleen Furman's body, but I walked along the river park until I saw yellow crime-scene tape. Shirley Thompson's car was parked across the street.

I found the reporter with her camera standing as close as she could get to where the cops had the Furman's position staked out. There were three paths tramped down in the snow. The cops and forensics people kept carefully to those paths.

"Any more revelations?" I asked as I came up behind Thompson. She jumped, and gave me a startled look.

"They arrested Dr. Sebastian Fernandez from the College," she said.

"I heard that. Any idea what she was doing out here? It was snowing, wasn't it?"

"Yes. All I've been able to find out, she had dinner with Fernandez. The last time anyone saw her was leaving the restaurant."

"Which one?"

"Chez Axel."

The same bistro where I had met Furman. I hadn't thought she enjoyed it that much.

"We're what, half, maybe three-quarters, of a mile from there? Kathleen didn't strike me as the outdoorsy let's-go-for-a-walk-in-the-snow kind of girl."

Thompson shook her head. "No, I don't think so. There weren't any tracks leading to where they found her. The snow covered everything."

It was still cloudy, and the temperature was below freezing. The ice and snow hadn't started to melt yet.

"Any idea where else she went yesterday?"

Thompson gave me a lopsided grin. "Aren't I the one who's supposed to be asking the questions?"

"I have what the cops told me, I figured I'd check it with what you've learned."

She tilted her head, obviously considering my offer. "Trade?"

"Someplace warm?"

We retired to a small bakery down the street. She ordered coffee, I ordered tea. I told her what information Barclay had shared with me, and she said that Furman had been seen at the Wayfarer Inn the previous afternoon.

"Any idea who she visited there?" I asked.

"No. I would guess Tomas Ortiz, or the Ariases, or Lieutenant Barclay. I don't know of anyone else staying there who might be connected to the Henderson story."

Maybe it shouldn't have bothered me, but the reporter saw Alice as a story, as did Kelly, the cops saw Alice as a case, the CIA saw her as a problem. I barely knew her, but when I thought of her, I got a feeling of uncontrolled terror. How horrifying it must have been to feel herself thrust out into space that far above the ground. For some reason, it really, really bothered me.

"You're the only other person I know who's staying there presently," I said.

"Yes, that's true." She snorted. "Hell, no one talks to me. I wonder if Lieutenant Kagan will arrest all of us next."

"I thought he had his culprit."

Thompson shook her head. "Keith Porter gave Dr. Fernandez a ride back to the College after he said good night to Ms. Furman."

"Oh?"

She suddenly looked a bit flustered. "Uh, well..."

"You saw them, but you haven't told the cops yet."

She blushed.

"Was Ms. Furman there at the time? I mean, maybe that was after Fernandez attacked her?"

Thompson bit her lip and looked down at her lap. When she raised her head, she said, "I think it was before she was attacked. Fernandez left her at the restaurant and walked to the Grand. Furman went the other direction."

"What time was that?"

"About eight-thirty."

The 'other direction' would take her toward Lowell's bookstore, which would have closed a couple of hours earlier. Otherwise, there were several bars on Main Street, mostly catering to locals or college students, and the Wayfarer Inn. The nightlife in Wicklow—even on a Friday night—was rather scant. I doubted she planned to hike out to the College.

"You don't suppose she had a lover here?" I asked.

"I never saw any indication of that. She almost always dines alone at the restaurant in the Grand."

Which was where she was staying. The most overpriced, pretentious place in town. But for a woman traveling alone, hotel restaurants always felt safer than going out. The restaurant at the Wayfarer was almost as good, and a lot cheaper.

"And you followed Fernandez," I said. "Why?"

"Tomas Ortiz told me about his history with Alice Henderson."

"You know that I'll have to tell the police about this."

She nodded and tried to look contrite. I wasn't fooled. I stood and tossed a five on the table.

"Don't worry about it," I said. "I don't think you have much competition for your scoop. Did you follow Porter and Fernandez?"

"No. I didn't want to drive in the snow."

"So, why do you think they went to the College?"

"I just assumed. That was the direction they went."

I walked out of the bakery and turned toward the police station. I called Barclay while I walked and told him about my conversation with the reporter.

"Where are you now?" he asked.

"On my way to tell Kagan."

"Lunch afterward?"

"Sure. Where?"

"I'll pick you up at the station."

I walked into the police department and asked the uniformed woman at the desk for Sam Kagan. He kept me waiting for about ten minutes.

"Dr. Robinson. What can I do for you today?"

"I spoke to Shirley Thompson. She tells me that she saw Dr. Fernandez and Kathleen Furman last night."

"Oh? Well, come on in."

He led me back to his office, which was only a little larger than his desk.

"So, where did she see them?"

"Leaving Chez Axel. She told me that they parted ways, and Sebastian went to the Grand, where he met with that

CIA agent, Keith Porter. Then Porter gave him a ride somewhere."

He thought about it. "And why was she following him?"

"The same reason she didn't come forward. She's working on a story. It wouldn't be any fun if she just told you Fernandez has an alibi. Better if she can break the story in the newspaper and be the hero."

Kagan gave me a baleful stare. "You have a very suspicious mind."

"She didn't deny it. Fernandez didn't say anything about meeting up with Porter?"

He shook his head. "I wonder why. Lord, it would be a mess if Porter was involved. And I will probably have to let Fernandez go."

"It's certainly not a secret that he and Porter are connected. I've seen Porter in Fernandez's office on campus."

"May I ask you how you ended up interrogating Shirly Thompson?"

"We were in the bakery over by the crime scene at the same time. She was feeling chatty. I think she hoped I might actually talk about Kelly's book, but she probably was disappointed."

"Well, I guess I need to talk to Porter."

"Good luck. He's a major asshole."

"I've noticed."

"What has Kathleen said? I mean, did she see her attacker?"

"She hasn't said anything yet. Still unconscious the last time I checked, and the doctors aren't being very cooperative."

CHAPTER 22

Lieutenant Barclay was waiting for me in the parking lot when I left the station. I could see exhaust from the tailpipe, so the engine was running. And when I got in, the car was warm. He put it in gear and pulled out of the lot in the direction of the College.

"Where are we going?" I asked.

"The Faculty Club. For lunch, they have a small tenderloin and a salad at a price my expense account and my waistline like. So, what did Lieutenant Kagan have to say?"

"That he planned to have a talk with Agent Porter, but he didn't relish doing it."

"Unfortunately, Sam seems to avoid confrontation, which isn't the best trait for a criminal investigator."

Barclay parked in the lot next to the library, and we entered the restaurant through the back entrance. Normally, I wouldn't expect the Faculty Club to be particularly busy for lunch on a Saturday, but it seemed the weather influenced the faculty and staff who lived on or near campus to stay close to home.

I noticed that the Faculty Club shared a supplier with

Carragher's. Unsurprising for a small town. The crab bisque on special sounded wonderful on a cold day.

We gave the waitress our orders, then James leaned forward and spoke in a quiet tone. The look on his face made me hope he might say something personal, but to my disappointment he stayed professional.

"Fernandez has an alibi? I'm not shocked. I am interested in what he and Furman discussed, and where Porter went after he dropped Fernandez off. Does Fernandez live on campus?"

I shook my head. "There's a neighborhood northeast of campus, southeast of the city. Custom-built homes on large lots. He lives alone except for a housekeeper, but she doesn't sleep there. A number of the senior professors and business owners in town have houses up there."

He raised an eyebrow, and I grinned.

"I don't have to be nosey: I just ask Kelly. She knows just about everything that's going on around here. If she doesn't, then Katy Bosun or Lowell Carragher probably do. They're both local, and they know where all the bodies are buried."

"And you just aggregate the information."

"Someone has to. Sam Kagan hasn't caught on to that step."

"All too often, he doesn't ask the right questions," Barclay said.

"As you said, he dislikes confrontation. I think you also probably need to talk to Agent Porter."

※

Barclay gave me a ride back into town, and dropped me near the Wayfarer Inn. I knew the night shift wouldn't be at work, but the reporter said that Furman had been there earlier in the day.

I bought a glass of wine and was one of only three customers, so the bartender was open to chatting. He knew who the Ariases were, and Tomas Ortiz, but he didn't recognize my description of Furman.

But as I left the bar, a waitress approached me.

"Uh, excuse me. You were asking about a woman? Was that the one who was killed last night?"

"She was attacked, but she didn't die. Have you seen her here?"

She nodded. "That's good. I saw her yesterday. She had an argument with that Spanish guy who's staying here?"

"Older? White hair and a cane?"

With a vigorous shake of her head, she said with a smile, "Oh, Señor Ortiz? No. He's such an old-fashioned gentleman. The younger guy. The one who's built like a fire hydrant and acts like he's angry all the time."

"He had an argument with the woman I described?"

"Right over there. It went on for about five minutes. By the end, he was red in the face and shouting at her. I couldn't hear the beginning, but the last thing he said was, 'You're protecting a murderer.' Then he went back into the hotel, and she walked toward town."

"Is that the only time you've seen her?"

"Oh, no. She's been here for dinner a couple of times. Lousy tipper."

I thanked her, handed her a five, and walked over to Lowell's bookstore.

"Good afternoon!" he called when I entered his shop. The cheerful exuberance was out of character.

"Why are you so chipper today?" I asked.

"I won a bet with myself. There was a suspicious near-death in town, and I bet that our local amateur detective would be out and about, sniffing for clues."

I sat down on the chair next to the counter.

"I'm not sure whether I should be offended."

He laughed. "I assume you've been out to the crime scene."

"Can't get near it. The cops are in a frenzy trying to catalog everything before it melts."

"Yes, I'm sure. So, to what do I owe the pleasure?"

"You've met Kathleen Furman, haven't you?"

"Of course. Stuck in a hotel room, night after night. Have you seen what they put on hotel TVs?"

"And what was she reading?"

"Normally, I wouldn't answer such a question. Client confidentiality and all that," he chuckled, "but considering the circumstances, I don't think she will object. Romances. In particular, historical romances set during the Witch Wars. Is that something you ever read?"

I shook my head.

"Well, then, telling you the authors' names probably wouldn't mean anything to you. The most recent book she bought was *Love Spell for a Duke*, and the one before that was *A Quiet Knight with the Sorcerer's Daughter*. Both by authors who write very sexy."

"That seems to fit with what I've learned. No romantic relationships while she was here."

"I don't think that was by choice. She was in here once with one of the CIA chaps. She seemed interested, but he seemed oblivious."

"Not an Ian Fleming type of spook."

"Not at all."

"I was told that she had an argument with Pablo Arias yesterday afternoon. He accused her of protecting a murderer."

"I'm afraid that anyone who is not actively working on jailing Sebastian Fernandez falls into that category. Maria seems quite concerned that her brother could be a target. And with Kathleen's attack, the bodies do seem to be piling up."

"I originally thought she was here to oversee the investigation and determine the cause of Agent Colby's death. But that wasn't something she was interested in, nor do I think she was qualified to do so."

"I'm not sure anyone involved in the investigation of any of the deaths is qualified. Except, perhaps, your friend Lieutenant Barclay."

"My father thinks highly of him, and he seems competent."

"And nice to look at?"

"I think so, yes."

"Do you have plans for Thanksgiving?"

I hadn't even thought of it, but it was November.

"No. Why?"

"Susan suggested I invite you out to the restaurant."

"Thank her for me, and tell her I am delighted."

"We usually have an intimate dinner with twenty or thirty of our closest friends." He winked at me. "If Lieutenant Barclay is still here, bring him along."

CHAPTER 23

Still feeling restless, I called Kelly. She was at home and invited me to drop by.

I trudged up the hill to her house. Most people had shoveled the sidewalks in front of their houses, but there were a few places where the path was slick and treacherous. The sky was still overcast and gray, and for the first time that year, I noticed that the days were growing shorter.

Walking along her street, I noted the neat little houses. Many of them resembled Kelly's home with their white picket fences. The snow was melting a little, but not enough to reveal the lawns and gardens surrounding the houses.

I reached Kelly's place—white with blue trim, and its picket fence. I raised my hand to wave at the figure standing at the back of the house, and then realized it wasn't Kelly. I stopped and watched for a moment, then saw the spark and fire.

I rushed through the gate, drawing my wand from inside my coat. The dark-coated figure didn't see me at first, but when he did, he immediately turned to run.

"Fulgur percutiens!"

Lightning flashed from my wand, striking the retreating

figure. I didn't bother to see what damage I might have done, turning my attention instead to the flames racing up the side of the building.

"*Exstinguere!*"

The spell worked, extinguishing the flame, but not quite in time. The metal gas can the arsonist left behind exploded, throwing me through the air. I landed hard on my back, my ears ringing and my sight rather fuzzy. I felt completely disoriented.

It took me some time to regain my senses, and I finally focused on Kelly's face, bending down above me.

"Savanna! Are you all right?"

"Uh...I think so. What happened?"

Then I remembered the man who tried to set her house on fire, and tried to struggle into a sitting position.

"Is he still there?"

She looked around. "Who?"

"The guy with the fire."

Straightening up, she seemed to see something and set off in the direction I had last seen the man. She stopped, looking at the ground, then walked over to the fence separating her property from the house next door.

"Who was it?" she asked when she came back.

"I'm not sure. He set a fire. Did he get away?"

"It seems so. There's a small circle of melted snow and blackened grass, with footsteps leading away."

"I didn't want to put enough power into the spell to kill him. I guess I pulled my punch too much. The tracks, they aren't size eighteen, are they?"

"No, different stalker."

She helped me to my feet, and I felt some pain in my left arm and thigh. Looking down, I saw a piece of red metal embedded in my leg. Several similar smaller pieces were sticking out of my leather coat. As far as I could tell, I was punctured only in two places. Something to take care of inside the house.

We found the gas can—or what was left of it—lying about thirty feet from the house. The smell of gasoline was powerful enough that there was no doubt about the source of the fire.

Kelly's neighbors on one side were peering over the fence, and a siren was growing louder.

"Someone tried to burn my house," Kelly said. "Suppose I had been asleep and you didn't come just when you did?"

"I wish I had a clear look at his face," I said. "I'd recognize the coat he was wearing. What surprises me is that he did it in broad daylight. Uh, look, do you think I can go inside so I can look at this shrapnel?"

"Oh, yeah, of course!"

She helped me limp into her back door, and sat me in one of the kitchen chairs. After retrieving a first aid kit from the bathroom, she went outside to talk to the firemen who had showed up.

I was wearing blue jeans over a pair of tights. Gritting my teeth, I pulled the chunk of steel out of my thigh. As I expected, that loosed a stream of blood, although it decreased the pain. I stood and quickly pulled down my pants and looked at the wound. A handful of paper napkins from the kitchen table helped staunch the flow.

"Do you have anything?" I asked Kelly when she walked back in the door. She breezed past me, went into the bathroom, and came out again.

I screamed—not loudly, but enough to let anyone in the house know I was concerned—when she poured isopropyl alcohol on my leg.

"Let's see what your arm looks like," she said.

"Your bedside manner needs some work," I said as I pulled the metal shard out of my arm and slipped out of my coat.

"Not part of my magic," she replied. "If you want a standard mother's care, I'm the one you come to. Would you like a bullet to bite?"

"About what I'd get from my mother. I didn't know it was standard."

"So, now you know why I have all these issues. TV's best-known kitchen witch has not a drop of healing magic, and absolutely no empathy. She never climbed a tree when she was a kid. I'm not sure she ever got dirty."

In spite of the pain, I snorted a laugh.

"Empathy and my mother never met," I said. "Any ideas who might want to burn down your house?"

"Off the top of my head? The CIA. Sorry bastards."

"I was afraid you'd say that."

An EMT showed up at that point, along with an arson investigator from the fire department, and a detective who wasn't Sam Kagan. They had a lot of questions. I gave the EMT priority.

<hr />

My phone woke me up. I was a bit groggy but aware that my thigh throbbed and there were several sharp pains in my arm and flank.

"Yeah?" I answered.

"What do you need me to bring you, and where do I find it?"

David Hamilton's voice. My first feeling was confusion, then kind of a warm feeling that he cared. I opened my eyes and saw there was faint light filtering through the blinds on the window. I wasn't in my own bed.

"Hang on. Let me wake up."

"Sorry."

I thought about what I needed to prevent infection and heal up the injuries I'd sustained. The EMT closed the worst of the damage in my leg with three stitches. The arm wound was too small to worry about. It got a band-aid.

"Tell Stephen I need a potion for infection and a directed local painkiller. He'll know what's necessary. He probably has them brewed."

"Are you okay? Do you need any clothes?"

"I think so. You woke me up."

"You're still at Kelly's?"

"Yeah. Stephen has a key to my apartment. A pair of jeans, maybe?"

There was a click, and the phone went dead.

I drifted back to sleep but woke up again to pounding at the front door. I pulled myself into a sitting position about the time Kelly walked in and flipped on the light.

"Your fan club is here."

"I didn't invite them."

She chuckled. David, Stephen, and Lowell crowded together in the hall behind her.

"What time is it?"

"Ten o'clock."

"You should have told them I died."

She stepped out of the doorway and the three men barged in.

"I'm alive," I said, "and the damage is fairly minor. Save your sympathies for Kelly's house."

The potion Stephen brought was just what I needed. Magically enhanced, it dulled the pain at the wound sites without knocking me out. The antibiotic cream I saved for when I changed the bandages. Altogether, seven pieces of the gas can had penetrated my jeans and coat, but the one in my thigh was the worst.

"So, tell me. What did the police discover?" I asked. "Nothing? Even with snow to help track the arsonist?"

"Pretty much," Lowell said. "But James Barclay told me they

found fingerprints on the gas can. No idea if that will lead anywhere."

"He was wearing gloves," I said. "I'm pretty sure he used magic to spark the fire."

They hung around for about an hour, then Kelly threw them out so we could get some sleep.

"The cops left two men to watch the house," Kelly said, and turned out the light.

"You need to move all your book stuff to the library," I told her. "Don't tempt them again."

CHAPTER 24

Someone knocking on the door woke me up. This time I could tell the sun was already shining.

"I was told that Dr. Robinson might be here," Lieutenant Barclay said when Kelly answered the door.

"Yes, she is. Come in. Would you like some coffee while I see if she's awake?"

"Thank you."

Kelly came into the room where I spent the night. I was already swinging my legs out of bed.

"Do you have a robe or something?" I asked. "I might have to send you over to my place to get me a dress. I don't think I can put my jeans on over this bandage."

She disappeared, then came back with a thick flannel robe and a pair of well-worn slippers.

"Coffee or tea?" she asked.

"Coffee, I think."

I put on the robe and slippers, and hobbled out to her living room.

"Good morning, Lieutenant. Are you up bright and early, or am I just a lie-abed?"

"I heard you were wounded in action but refused to go to the hospital."

"And what would that do to my credibility if my students found out I believed in the pharmaceutical companies more than my own medicines? My coat protected me from most of the shrapnel, and the piece in my thigh wasn't very large and only hit muscle."

"You weren't the only one who was lucky to be wearing a coat."

He picked up a shopping bag I hadn't noticed and pulled a coat from it. Suede, with sheep wool lining – either fake or real, I couldn't tell. The coat looked like it had been in a fire. Especially the back of it was obviously scorched, and it looked as though a very large cat had used it as a scratching post.

"Does this look familiar?" Barclay asked.

"You caught him?"

He shook his head. "No, we found this thrown near some garbage cans on the next street over. I figure he was afraid it made him too noticeable. What I can't figure is how he was walking at all."

"I only gave him a small one. I hoped to capture him, not kill him."

"Dr. Robinson, how strong is your magic?"

I shrugged. "I'm lethal, if that's what you're asking. I wouldn't consider carrying a gun to protect myself. But I'm not going to be blowing up Howard Hall or the Vatican."

"That's a relief. As to possible suspects, this coat wouldn't fit Sebastian Fernandez."

"The suspect ran, Lieutenant. I would be surprised if Fernandez can run. But to answer the question you haven't asked, no, I didn't see his face. Yes, I'm sure it was a man. Lowell told me last night that you found fingerprints on the gas can."

"From at least seven different people. None of whom match

anyone on the National Crime database. Of course, we haven't managed to find all the pieces."

"How about the government personnel office?"

"For some reason, the personnel records of members of our intelligence services are classified."

"I take it the can wasn't purchased locally."

"Nope. Best thing about this mess is that the damage to Kelly's house is minimal. Whatever you did to smother the flame worked very well."

"Magic."

※

We helped Kelly gather all her papers, computers, and anything of Alice's and box them up. James carried the boxes out to his car.

After that, Kelly and James bundled me into his car and drove me home. I made them stop by the only place that was open that early and get breakfast to go. Once we arrived at the College, they helped carry the food in, and I set the table for the three of us.

"I have a bottle of champagne and a bottle of orange juice. Can I interest you in mimosas as well as tea?" I asked.

"I'm on duty," James said.

"No, he's not. And if he wants to be boring, you and I can drink his share," Kelly said with a laugh.

I had missed dinner the previous day, so I dug into the large breakfast without any shame. Once my stomach stopped growling at me, I took a long pull at my mimosa and a sip of tea, then leaned back in my chair.

"So, what have we learned in the past day or two? Someone is getting impatient. Tried to kill Kathleen Furman, burn down Kelly Grace's house—and maybe kill her, too. Would that be the same person? Or are these two different bad guys? How are

Furman's activities and Kelly's book connected in a way that both must be silenced? I would think they are on two different sides of the issue."

"Very good questions," James said. "I can easily drum up suspects for the arson. What has Furman done to piss someone off?"

"The only people I can think of is Porter and the CIA guys, or Pablo Arias," I said. "That's assuming Fernandez had some reason after his dinner with her, and the CIA got jumpy."

"And Porter's reason?" Kelly asked.

"Something she said during that dinner. We further assume that the interests of the U.S. Government align with those of Fernandez and his friends on the Council, but we don't know that for sure."

Kelly took a sip of her mimosa. "Something Alice said to me once was that no one's interests ever aligned completely. She had a story about a lover of hers in East Germany who worked for British Intelligence. She said she couldn't prove it, but she was convinced that the U.S. intelligence apparatus outed him to the Stasi, who of course killed him. The lesson being that she couldn't trust anyone."

"We shouldn't assume that Furman is here to protect Fernandez, or that her interests align with the CIA," I said. "She is here to protect her mentor in Santa Fe."

"And we don't know anything about Fernandez's relationships with anyone in Washington," James said.

"Would her control in Santa Fe sacrifice his own agent?" I shook my head. "I think either she learned something she shouldn't have, or she threatened to do or reveal something."

After James and Kelly left, taking the documents to the College library, I gave my leg a dose of a magical painkiller, took a bath, and sat by my window. The snow was melting a little, but the temperature was still very cold.

My thoughts were with Kathleen Furman. Clearly, the

woman was out of her depth, but I couldn't imagine why someone would feel the need to kill her. I would have been far less surprised if Shirley Thompson turned up dead. I hoped that she took Furman's assault as a warning. Someone was very concerned about their secrets.

CHAPTER 25

A knock on my door woke me. That was becoming an irksome habit, but at least I was in my own bed. I threw on a nightgown and a robe, then limped to my outer door.

"Good morning," Barclay said, handing me a takeout coffee. I let him in, although I was tempted to take the coffee and shut the door in his face. I was warm and cozy in bed, and I didn't have a single thing I had to do or a place to go.

"And to what do I owe the pleasure?" I asked as I led him through my entryway.

"I've come to ask you a favor."

Such words are always a warning.

"The answer is no."

The startled look on his face caused me to burst out laughing.

"Oh, come on, Lieutenant. You should know better than to start a conversation like that at this time of the morning."

He had the grace to look sheepish.

"Yes, I probably should. Look, I'm trying to talk Kelly into postponing this book. Let things cool down, and wait until all the murder investigations are complete. Is it going to make that much difference if she publishes Alice's book in the spring, or a year from then?"

I dropped into my favorite chair, took the lid off the coffee, smelled it, and took a sip. Some sort of caramel latte. Since I considered the chain that sold such concoctions an abomination, I took the sip to be polite and sat it down on a coaster.

"You're not going to get any help from me," I said. "Besides, don't you think it's rather stupid to ask that of her? With all this crap going on, she's not getting any work done on the book anyway. It will probably take her a month to sort and organize things before she can start work again. Besides, after she finishes it, the publisher will take a year to edit it and print it. These things don't happen overnight."

I thought about it for a minute. "I'll tell you what. Get her a paid leave of absence, a free place to live in Santa Fe, and let her work on the book down there."

He shook his head and sat down.

"I had a feeling that would be your answer," he said.

"What I can't figure out is why everyone thinks I have any influence over a grown woman whom I've only known for a few months? Okay, here's another plan. I'll call my mother, get Kelly a place there to work on the book, and no one will have to worry about her."

He was looking down at his coffee. His eyes raised slowly to my face.

"I can't tell if you're joking or not."

"You wouldn't have to worry about the CIA or Marcus LePage or Sebastian Fernandez. All you'd have to do is dispose of the bodies when they're thrown over the wall."

He studied my face for a while. "You aren't joking."

"No, but I'm not sure if I could talk Mom into taking Kelly. It would make it easier if she thought it would piss off the Council and my father."

"I'm not even touching that."

"Wise man. My suggestion is to let Kelly work on the book in the library here, assign her a bodyguard or two, and figure out who the homicidal maniac or maniacs are. I can cast a set of wards around her house to protect it." I thought about it for a minute. "I'm willing to bet that moving Keith Porter and his boys to somewhere like Buffalo or Fargo would be a good way to start sorting this mess."

Barclay sighed and slid down in his seat.

"If I only had the power..."

"Any more news on Furman, now that you've thawed her out? What time was she attacked?"

"Well, she wasn't frozen, but the cold might have helped mitigate her injuries. Around nine-thirty in the evening. The kids who found her evidently interrupted things, and the forensics team says they measured the snow on her body against the depth of the snow on the grass around her. Her body was still warm, although she was mildly hypothermic."

"So, nobody has an alibi. Porter, Fernandez, Arias, Ortiz, you, me, Kelly. Right? We were all at home, alone, watching television."

He started to say something, then barked out a laugh. "You're probably right. Except for you. You don't have a TV."

"Silly man. I have a computer and a Netflix subscription."

"Well, they think that bruise on her head was from a blow, not a fall. She also had a large bruise in the middle of her back. They speculate the attacker knelt on her."

"So much simpler to use magic, like with Colby."

"Is the snow melted at the place she was assaulted?"

"Yes. A couple of forensics people are scouring the area—in case some evidence was hidden by the snow."

"What do you have going on this morning?" I asked. "I assume you're rather at loose ends, since you're rousting innocent civilians at the crack of dawn."

"I'm at your disposal."

"Do you coppers ever scry murder scenes? It seems to me it would be very helpful."

Barclay shook his head. "The evidence would be inadmissible. The accuracy is questionable, so it might also influence the investigation in the wrong way."

"And truth spells are considered a form of coercion."

"Not really, but in this country, it's unconstitutional. Fifth amendment, you know. Self-incrimination and all that."

"Pity. Look, let me treat my leg, then I'll make breakfast, and you can drive me downtown. I'd like to look at the scene when I'm not freezing."

CHAPTER 26

Three police cars—two marked cars and one I recognized as Sam Kagan's—were parked at the Wayfarer Inn when we drove by.

"What's going on there?" I asked.

"No idea," Barclay answered and turned the corner. He drove around the block and found a parking space next to the café.

I hung back to let him take the lead. The way things had been going, I hoped there wasn't another murder.

What we found were the cops, the hotel manager, the Arias twins, and Shirley Thompson in the lobby. The manager, a tall, thin man with dark hair, was telling the cops that he wanted Pablo and Shirley out of the hotel, and he didn't care how.

The manager, Pablo, and Shirley were all talking—yelling really—at the same time, Pablo switching between English and Spanish, although I couldn't tell if anyone other than his sister spoke Spanish. A tall, husky police sergeant occasionally tried to get a word in. Kagan didn't appear to be doing anything useful.

Barclay assessed the scene, asked Kagan a couple of questions, then shouted for everyone to be quiet. He sent Pablo and Kagan to one side, the sergeant and the hotel manager to another side, and took Thompson to a third part of the lobby. I moved in to comfort Maria, who was obviously upset.

"Pablo so angry," she told me.

"Yes, I can see that. What happened?"

She gestured toward Thompson. "Questions, questions. No go away."

The three cops got together and compared the stories they had heard. I edged closer to eavesdrop.

"It sounds like the easiest solution is to send Thompson on her way and bar her from the premises," Barclay said. "The Ariases' rooms are being paid by the College, and the manager doesn't want to harm that relationship. Sound about right?"

"Mr. Arias probably won't be a problem if the reporter isn't harassing him," Kagan said.

The sergeant nodded in agreement.

I motioned to Pablo, who came over to where Maria and I were standing.

"Take your sister upstairs, and stay there," I told him. "And stay away from that reporter."

"I try to. She won't leave us alone."

He took his sister's arm, and they went to the elevator. Barclay was talking to Thompson, and the other cops were talking to the manager, who was nodding his head.

"You can't keep me from asking someone questions," Thompson said as I approached.

"The hotel will take out a restraining order," Barclay replied. "As this is private property, they have a right to protect the privacy of their guests, and the manager can file a complaint that you are disturbing the peace. Now, I'm sure you don't want to take things that far, so I suggest you pack your bags and move to another hotel."

Which is what she did in the end.

After she loaded her bags in her car and drove away, James and I continued our drive down to the riverside park. The crime-scene tape was still up, but there weren't any people in forensics coveralls wandering around.

"So, what do you expect to discover here?" he asked. "We can't disturb the scene."

I wanted to tell him that he was too tied to police procedure, but I bit my tongue. I got out of the car and walked around the perimeter. Where the body was found was still staked out.

"Where do you think she came from?" I asked, motioning in the direction of the Grand Hotel. "Down the walkway? There are only three possibilities, right? She was followed, she was ambushed by someone waiting for her, or she happened to run into someone by accident."

Barclay stood, rubbing his chin, and surveyed the scene.

"But who would be here? Waiting for her with homicide in mind? How would someone know she was coming here? And you missed a fourth possibility. She could have come here accompanied by the murderer."

"It is on the way to the Wayfarer," I said.

"A long way to walk. She left her rental car at the Grand. Considering the weather, I would guess she planned to meet someone. If she walked to the Wayfarer, she would have to walk back as well."

"She was wearing high heels?" I asked.

"Yes. Not the best footwear for the weather."

I motioned at the road that ran along the park.

"If Porter gave Fernandez a lift home, he would have driven by here on his way back to the Grand Hotel."

Barclay nodded. "He might have seen her when he passed here, then seen her again on his way back."

"Or Fernandez could have seen her, got his own car after Porter dropped him off, and come back."

Barclay chuckled. "Or they both could have tried to murder her. One held her down while the other silenced her."

"I think it was little green aliens."

"That makes as much sense as anything else we've talked about."

I pulled a canvas bag out of my coat pocket and began walking around the perimeter, just outside the crime-scene tape, dribbling salt on the ground.

"What are you doing?" he asked.

"Just want to look at things from a different perspective," I replied.

The size of space they had marked off was fairly large, and I had only brought two bags of salt with me, so any spell I cast wouldn't be wholly confined. But I could define a space and make an effort to see any psychic shadows within that space.

When I finished sketching out the ring—which was far larger than I would have liked due to Barclay refusing to allow me inside the crime-scene tape—I pulled a collapsible tripod from my bag and set it on the sidewalk at the end of the circle closest to town. On top of it, I placed a shallow steel bowl, about a foot in diameter, cast a ward on the surface of it, then filled the bowl with a mixture of iron oxide, chemical-grade salt, aluminum powder, and finally a long ribbon of magnesium.

Barclay watched me, and said, "I vaguely remember my alchemy classes. What you're doing isn't exactly legal, is it?"

"Just a little harmless chemistry, Lieutenant." I cast another ward around the bowl. "Harmless being relative, of course. Without the ward to contain the flame, it isn't something you want a child mixing in the garage."

I pulled my wand from my sleeve, then lit the magnesium. The fire in the pan, contained by the ward, leapt three feet in the air, white hot.

"*Revelare praeterita! Decimo quinto Novembris ad horam nonam vesperi!*" I said, directing the spell through my wand into the flame.

The area inside the flame turned from eye-searing white to clear. Barclay moved to stand by my shoulder. Inside the window I had created was the same scene as we had before I lit the flame, but it was night.

"And?" he asked.

"We just have to be patient and watch. You said the time of the attack was between nine and nine-thirty. I hope it wasn't much later than that, or I'll have to cast the spell again. I only brought enough material for the flame to burn for about an hour."

"What exactly is that flame? What are you burning?"

"Witchfire. Modern chemistry and our military call it thermite. Very easy to make, actually, but rather dangerous without the ward to contain it. You could use another material, but it wouldn't burn as hot, or give you as clear a picture. During the Witch Wars, it was loaded up in trebuchets and used against castle walls."

We watched for about fifteen minutes. It started snowing lightly, and then a woman appeared—we saw her back as though she came from our perspective. She was attempting to run, but a tight skirt and high heels limited her to a stumbling trot. When she glanced over her shoulder, we saw that it was Kathleen Furman, and the expression on her face showed fear.

A man in a long, dark, bulky coat and a dark stocking cap appeared behind her, and he was running. When he caught up with her, he ran into her. She fell, and hit her head as he dropped to his knees, landing on her back. He grabbed her hair and slammed her forehead into the pavement.

All of that was silent, as was his escape. He searched in her purse, lifted out a small spiral notebook and a hotel key, then hurriedly walked off toward the street and out of our field of vision. Furman lay there, and the snowfall turned heavier, covering her body.

I knew there probably was nothing left to see, but I had to wait for the thermite to finish burning. I couldn't tear my eyes away from her body. Then two more people entered the scene. One of them knelt down beside Kathleen, and the other took a few steps back and pulled a cell phone out of her pocket and started tapping on its screen.

"I never saw his face," I said of the attacker.

"No, I didn't either. The angle was wrong, and we only saw his back."

"At least you have an exact time," I said.

"Yes. Nine-seventeen."

"I don't think it was Sebastian Fernandez."

"Don't discount magic, Dr. Robinson. My information is that both Porter and Fernandez can cast illusions."

"What kind of illusion would make it look like Fernandez could run? The man weighs well over three hundred pounds. That little notebook was what she always wrote her notes in when she interviewed someone. What about her phone? I didn't see him take it."

Barclay nodded. "He left her phone, oddly enough. I think Fernandez was indiscreet at their last meeting, and the CIA boys cleaned up his mess. Whoever it was took her hotel key and her car keys, so we're stuck with whatever she tells us when she wakes up."

CHAPTER 27

"The doctors say she has a small fracture in her forehead and they've drilled a hole to drain a hematoma on her brain," Sam Kagan said. "She also has two broken vertebrae in her back. She didn't die, but not for lack of effort by her attacker."

I was sitting in the hospital waiting room with James Barclay and Kagan. It had been two days since Kathleen Furman was attacked.

"Has she woken up at all?" I asked.

"No. They are keeping her sedated on purpose until the swelling in her brain goes down," Kagan said.

"And have they brought in a healer?"

"There are two very good ones on staff here, both also medical doctors," he replied. "This is Wicklow, Dr. Robinson. We have more healers than preachers here."

"Other than us, has anyone inquired about her?" I asked.

Kagan shook his head. "I have spoken with the doctors and the nursing staff. No one sees her without my permission, and they aren't to divulge anything about her condition. Ongoing criminal case. But no, none of the obvious suspects have tried to check on her. Except for the rummaging of her room, it might have been a mugging. But a mugger would have taken her purse. Credit cards and one hundred and eighty-seven dollars in cash."

"Have you spoken to any of the obvious suspects?" Barclay asked.

Kagan hesitated, then said, "Yes, I spoke with Dr. Fernandez. He didn't know why she was out walking, although he said he did see her on the street when Keith Porter gave him a ride home.."

"But you haven't spoken to Porter?"

"Not yet."

"Have you managed to unlock her phone?"

Kagan gestured toward Barclay. "The State boys have it. A little beyond our capabilities here in Wicklow."

Barclay and I left, and as we walked down the stairs to the parking lot, he said, "I wonder when he plans to speak with Porter?"

"Detecting is an exhaustive business, and not one to be rushed into," I replied.

He shook his head. "You can be mean sometimes."

I smiled and winked at him. "I like Sam Kagan, but lazy people irritate me. Sam is not just physically lazy, but intellectually lazy. I have students like him all the time. I want to just shake them until they get a clue."

When we reached the parking lot, Barclay asked, "Other than the spooks, who else might want to silence her?"

I shrugged. "We know that Pablo Arias isn't a fan. Maybe she has an ex that followed her here, waiting for his chance at revenge."

Barclay shook his head. "Any exes she has want more distance. I doubt she ever broke anyone's heart."

"And you accuse me of being mean?"

"I'm a strong empath," he said, "and that woman is very, very needy."

A familiar car pulled into the lot, and Shirley Thompson got out.

"Another soon-to-be-disappointed interviewer of Kathleen," I said.

"So it appears. Can I drop you anywhere?"

"And where are you off to?"

"Speak with Maria and Pablo Arias. As you said, they might have a motive."

"In that case, drop me by Lowell's bookstore."

To my surprise, I found Kelly at the bookstore.

"Maria is going back to Argentina," she announced when I came in. "I need to interview her before she leaves, and Lowell and I were just discussing when we could do that."

"Has all the legal paperwork been taken care of?" I asked.

She nodded. "Yes. She's very anxious to get back to her daughter, and I get the feeling her husband is pressuring her."

"But Pablo is going to stay?"

"He says he'll stay until Fernandez is locked up for the murder of his mother."

Lowell rolled his eyes.

"Has anyone told him how long court proceedings take in this country?" I asked.

"So, anyway," Kelly said, turning to Lowell, "When can you translate for me?"

"Tomorrow," Lowell said. "Let's make it about ten o'clock out at the resort, why don't we? Less distractions out there, and leave Pablo here. He would be the only one talking, and Maria will sit like a mouse in the corner."

"Would either of you know why Pablo is so angry with that reporter, Shirley Thompson?" I asked. "I would think he would want to talk to her."

Kelly chuckled. "She keeps asking him for proof of his allegations against Dr. Fernandez. Her editor doesn't want to get sued." She stood, put her coat on, picked up her purse, and said, "As pleasant as the company and the warmth are, I have things I need to do. See you tomorrow."

I took her seat next to the counter.

"Tea?" Lowell asked.

"Please. I'm not used to this weather."

He went into the back room and came back with a steaming mug with the tag from a tea bag hanging out of it.

"You should sell some pastries and tea," I said. "Like that big-chain bookstore across the river."

"You mean the place that's going out of business, leaving me with a big hole in my mall space? I did consider putting in a bakery next door here, but I think the shoe repair place is more stable. Have you heard anything about Kathleen Furman?"

"She's still out, but the doctors are saying she'll pull through. Another day or two before she's going to answer any questions."

CHAPTER 28

Kelly asked me to go along for her interview with Maria.
"She seems to relax more in your presence. I'm not sure why," she told me.

It wasn't a difficult decision. She offered to buy me lunch, and I would eat at Carragher's Retreat daily if I could.

Barclay and Kelly came by and picked me up at eleven in the morning, then we swung by the Wayfarer and Maria joined us.

I had noticed that either Maria's English was improving or she managed to overcome her shyness when no one was available to translate for her. She and Kelly sat in the back seat and made small talk, commenting on the countryside we passed.

Since encountering an illusion on that road, I was always a little tense driving out to the resort. We came around a corner to find a large tree fallen across the road. I whipped out my wand and cast a banish-illusion spell. Nothing happened.

"It's real!" I yelled, bracing for impact even as James slammed on the brakes and tried to steer to the left.

The car slid into the tree with a loud crash, and the airbags went off. I sat there stunned, then looked over at James.

"Are you all right?"

"I think so," he said.

"Does your door work?" My door was definitely out of commission, pressed at least six inches past the edge of my seat toward me.

He tried his door and managed to push it open with a wrenching scream of metal-on-metal.

"Maria?" he asked as he got out.

"I am okay," she said. She opened her door, and James helped by grasping the handle and pulling on it.

"Kelly?" I asked.

"She not good," Maria said.

I unlatched my seat belt and crawled over the console. Looking into the back seat, I saw that the side airbag had deployed and knocked Kelly sideways on the seat. She was pale, and her right arm seemed to hang at an unnatural angle.

"Kelly?" I said louder. "Hey, you all right?"

"Uh. Not good," she responded weakly.

I scrambled out of the driver's side door and went around to where James was reaching into the back seat.

"I can't reach her seat belt," he said.

"Let me try. I'm smaller." I crawled in, released her seat belt, and pressed two fingers against the pulse in her throat. It was thready, but steady.

"How's your arm?"

"Hurts."

"Where?"

"Between the elbow and shoulder."

I cast a containment ward on her upper arm to hold it stationary, then grabbed her under her other arm and pulled her toward me. Once I was out of the car, James helped me and then carried her to the side of the road. I checked her legs and torso, but she didn't complain of pain anywhere except the arm. I pulled a small vial from my purse and held it to her lips.

"Drink this. It will help with the pain."

James called 911, and I called Susan at the resort.

"Susan? Savanna Robinson. There's a tree down on the road out to your place. You should warn any of your guests that the road is closed."

"Our road or the highway?"

"The highway, about a mile or maybe a little less from your turnoff."

"Thanks. I'll need to call people with reservations and tell them also. How big a tree? I can send the boys out with a chainsaw."

"We hit it. Pretty big tree, and a crashed sedan. I think it's going to take a wrecker."

"Savanna, one of our cooks just said that he came through there less than half an hour ago and the road was clear."

I hung up and turned to Barclay. "I think one of us should check how this happened."

"I agree," he said. "Are you sure you're all right?"

I wasn't but I nodded. "Yeah, I'm fine."

He pulled me into a hug. It was unexpected, but he was warm and solid, and I didn't resist. Then he stepped back, producing his wand and a pistol from inside his jacket. "And since I'm the one with a badge, you stay with Kelly."

I watched him jump the ditch on the side of the road and follow the tree trunk into the woods. While I waited on him, a truck came from the other direction and stopped on the other side of the tree.

"Are you folks all right?" Lowell called.

I walked around to where we could see each other.

"I think Kelly has a broken arm. We're waiting for an ambulance from town." I motioned toward the forest. "Lieutenant Barclay went to check things out."

Lowell crawled over the tree and inspected the car. Afterward, he knelt down by Kelly and spoke with her. The potion I gave her had kicked in, and she looked better.

I walked to the side of the road, trying to see James in the forest. The tree extended at least twenty or thirty feet past the ditch along the edge of the road, but I couldn't see him at all. I waited a few more minutes, then he seemed to appear out of thin air and walked toward me.

"The tree was uprooted, as though it was blown over," he said. "But we haven't had any strong winds, and none of the other trees seem to have been affected. I don't see anything natural that might have caused it."

"Let me go take a look," I said, walking past him. He turned to follow me.

His report was accurate. The soil around and on the tree's roots was fairly dry, and the root structure was solid. It would have taken a major amount of magical force to knock the tree over.

"Did you see any tracks?" I asked.

He pointed to the heavy layer of old leaves covering the ground. "Maybe if we had a dog out here. But nothing that I can see."

"I'm starting to get paranoid," I said.

"I can understand why."

"When I called the restaurant, Susan said one of her staff drove through here half an hour ago and the road was clear. Whoever did this had to park somewhere close. And unless they took the long way around, we would have passed them as they drove back to town."

"We only passed two cars and an old pickup coming out here," he said.

"The old pickup was probably an illusion covering one of those large American cars Porter and his friends drive. They don't seem to have any concerns about collateral damage, do they? How did they know it was us who would be first on the scene?"

"Coming the other way, we could see the tree in plenty of

time to stop," Lowell said, coming up behind us. "Unless, of course, you were one of the teenagers in the area."

"We'll never prove who did it," James said.

I knew he was right. The sound of an ambulance siren grew closer to us.

CHAPTER 29

The paramedics evaluated Kelly and found that her entire right side was bruised. They stabilized her arm and loaded her into the ambulance. Then they came for me.

"I'm fine," I said.

"No, you're not," Barclay told me. "You're limping and favoring your right arm."

"Well, I'm a little bit sore, but nothing's broken."

They all gave up, eventually, since I wasn't being cooperative. I did surreptitiously down a dose of the potion I gave Kelly.

Susan's son cut the tree into three pieces, and then he and Lowell, with some help from Barclay, ran a chain around the center part that was blocking the road. They used the truck to drag the log off to the side, leaving Barclay's car sitting forlornly in the road.

"I think you're going to need a new car," I said.

"This is ridiculous," he answered.

After the cops finished their investigation, and the wrecker towed the car back to town, Lowell loaded James, Maria, and me in the truck, and we drove to the resort.

I gave Maria a potion, and Susan provided a room where she could lie down. She was pretty shaken up but not injured.

"At least it didn't come down on the car," Lowell said as we sat down in the restaurant.

I glowered at him, but it didn't seem to bother him at all.

"Seriously," he continued, "doesn't all this seem to be a bit over the top? Alice killed, that CIA guy's dead, Kathleen Furman almost killed, someone tried to burn Kelly's house, and now this? I'm having a difficult time thinking this is all about Sebastian Fernandez and Operation Condor forty years ago."

Susan came by and took our orders—we were definitely late for lunch—and went back to the kitchen.

"So, what are you thinking?" James asked.

"I think we need to go through Alice's papers and find what everyone is so worried about. Think about it. Operation Condor is public knowledge. Savanna had no trouble finding that there's a warrant for Sebastian's arrest in Argentina. What is the bombshell waiting to be revealed?"

"I sort of asked that early on, after Alice's death," I said. "Kelly and I brainstormed it, and while Alice engaged with some politicians and high government officials, that was at least thirty years ago. Her affair with a senator was closer to fifty years ago, and he's dead."

"So, what might be in her files about Operation Condor that hasn't ever come to light?" Lowell asked.

"Or who was involved in the death squads who is now in a sensitive position?" James returned.

I thought about it. "Like a CIA or State Department operative on the ground in the early nineteen eighties, who is a senator or CIA director or something like that now?"

"Exactly," James said. "Or some kind of enabling document from the U.S. that implicates us far deeper in Condor than anyone has ever let on."

"You know," Lowell said, "a lot of Nazis fled to South

America after the war. I wonder if Alice knew about Stasi criminals who also fled there. But that would have occurred after she had already left Argentina."

"Do either of you know anything about codes?" I asked. "Kelly found a sheet of paper with what I'm convinced is the key to decipher coded documents. But so far, we haven't found a document that we think is encoded."

"And it may not look that way," Lowell said. "It may be something that appears totally innocuous."

"Kelly also said that Alice had documents and letters in at least four different languages."

Lowell nodded. "I do know someone who is a code-cipher expert. He lives somewhere in the San Francisco area, I think. Do you suppose I could see this page you suspect is a key?"

"We can ask Kelly for it."

About that time, Sam Kagan showed up. He sat down with us, and when Susan came over with a menu, just ordered a cup of coffee.

"That treefall doesn't look very natural, does it?" he said.

We all shook our heads.

"Does anyone have any suggestions as to where I should look for the source of all our excitement lately?"

"I think we need an exorcism," I said. "Get rid of all the spooks, and see where we stand."

He gave me a bit of a sour look, then took a deep breath.

"Unfortunately, no one with the authority to tell them to leave seems to want to exercise that authority."

"Sam, you and James are too constrained in your thinking," I said. "Fire with fire?"

Lowell burst out laughing. "Sometimes I think that our Dr. Robinson was born a bit too late. You would have fit in quite well in the seventeenth century."

"It's my mother's influence. She believes our thin veneer of civilization shouldn't allow barbarians to rage unhindered. The local representatives of the CIA's Supernatural Investigations Unit seem to have gone rogue. We can enter a formal complaint with their superiors, or we can fight back. But people are dying, and that tree stunt has stretched my sense of humor past the breaking point."

"I can't turn a blind eye to a mage battle in the middle of downtown," Kagan said.

"Not a problem. I can murder them in their beds."

Kagan and Barclay stared at me, obviously unsure if I was serious. Lowell burst out laughing.

"Or just let me fix their breakfasts some morning."

"Whoever sent them will just send more agents," Barclay said.

I shrugged. "There can't be an endless supply of idiots. Sooner or later they'll send someone with more brains than ego, and we can have a rational conversation."

"What we need to do is figure out why they're being sent," Lowell said. "Alice's book."

※

Lowell gave Maria and me a ride back to town, and Barclay rode back with Kagan. Lowell took us by the hospital, where we discovered Kelly had just been released. We found her in the hospital lobby. Her right arm was in a cast from her shoulder to below her elbow, and a strap from the upper arm, across her chest, under her other arm, and around her back held the broken arm against her torso. Her hand was free.

"They're telling me three to six weeks before I can start physical therapy for range of motion," she said. "No skiing for this kid this winter."

We dropped Maria at the Wayfarer, where a frantic Pablo was blaming everyone from God to Wicklow College to the government for putting his sister in danger. Kelly was in no condition to interview Maria, so that was postponed for a few days.

When we took Kelly to her house, I said, "We—Lowell, Barclay, and I—were hoping to get a copy of that page with the code key."

She nodded. "I do have a copy of it in my office. The doctors want me to take it easy for a couple of days, but I'll dig it out as soon as I'm back at work."

And when Lowell took me home, I started running water for a bath, and drank a couple of potions before undressing. My right shoulder and hip were deeply bruised. I knew I should probably get in an ice bath instead of a hot one, but I ignored my own advice. The hot bath and a glass of red wine were far more comfortable.

CHAPTER 30

Kelly called me when she went back to work.

"Hi, I have that code key page, or whatever it is. Want to come and get it?"

I chuckled. "I'm not sure. Let me arrange an armed escort. You wouldn't happen to remember what was with that page, would you? I mean, what papers it was stored with?"

"Yes, as a matter of fact. When you told me it was the key to a code, I kept the original with the other papers in that box. There were several letters, some documents, and a bunch of newspaper clippings. Do you want me to dig those out, too? I didn't really see anything there that would help me with the book."

"Yes. I'm going to bring Lowell and James along with me. Lowell says he knows a cryptographer who might be able to shed some light on that code thing. I'm not sure when I can round them up, but I'll call before we come."

Lowell had to call someone from the resort to come and take care of the bookstore, and James was in Pittsburgh getting a new car from the State Police office there. It was almost four o'clock in the afternoon before we made it to Kelly's office.

I could tell that the cast was going to cause her ongoing problems in doing even routine daily chores.

"Here's the box," she said, handing me what looked like an old shoebox. "I copied everything, but perhaps there's something about the original papers that has some meaning, so there they are."

I looked in the box, then restored the lid. I figured we could go through it later.

"Do you still want to do the interview with Maria?" Lowell asked. "She's flying back to Argentina on Monday." That was in five days.

"Yes, I do. Can you arrange things with her, Lowell? Maybe we could do it at your shop after hours."

"I'll see what I can do. Do you need a ride home?"

"Dr. Phillips is giving me a ride, but thanks."

We walked out, with me carrying the box.

"What do we do with this?" I asked. "For all we know, the contents of this mark me for automatic assassination just because I saw it."

Lowell laughed. "For all we know, the contents may be irrelevant. Maybe we need to steam the layers of cardboard for the secrets of the universe."

"Give Lowell a copy of the code sheet, and I'll take the box," James said.

"If you're going to ward the thing, I think it's probably safer in my place than a hotel," I said. "You might have noticed that the buildings here at the college were built to withstand a magical siege. I planned to put it in my alchemist's safe. I figure anything that will keep college students out will withstand the efforts of our terribly incompetent spooks."

"She has a point," Lowell said. "I suppose you could lay an archivist's ward on top of that, but I doubt it would be necessary."

They accompanied me home, and I took them to my

alchemy lab next door. I opened the safe, put the box inside, and closed it, then renewed the wards.

"What all do you keep in there?" James asked.

"Enough poisons to cleanse the Allegheny basin of all life—both fauna and flora—my diary, and the exam questions for the rest of the trimester. And the recipe for my banana bread."

They both laughed.

"In all seriousness, I don't keep a diary, and I'll give the banana bread recipe to anyone who asks. I do keep my mother's legacy locked up. That's not something that should fall into the wrong hands."

Lowell cocked his head, his brow furrowed. "Your mother?"

"Oh, surely you must know," I said. "I thought you were the most literate man in the country. You've never googled me?"

Barclay chuckled.

I shrugged. "My mother is Margaret McKenzie." The head of the Scottish Coven, the main non-Council witches' organization in Europe and North America. The coven that helped to destroy the English Empire and the Roman Catholic Church. Of course, that was hundreds of years before mother was born.

"Dear Goddess," Lowell breathed.

"Yes, Mad Maggie McKenzie. And my father is Seth Robinson. The two of them could barely stand to be in the same room with each other when I graduated university. I was afraid the place would ignite."

And I hoped my mother lived for a thousand years, so that I never had to face the problem of her succession. Maggie McKenzie was the most notorious witch in the world, and the main counter-balance to the Witches' Council that oversaw the use of magic and the relationships between witches and the non-magical.

"My mother is, to put it gently, not maternal. When I was three, she showed up in Santa Fe, handed me to my father, and told him that I was his problem. After that, I lived with Seth and spent my summers at Sterling Castle with Maggie. We all survived."

"You do have a bit of your mother's attitude," Lowell said.

"Have you met my mother?"

"As a matter of fact, on several occasions. We got along fairly well."

That caused me to chuckle. "I can see that. When can you contact your buddy in San Francisco?"

"I already have. He's in Santa Cruz, actually. I'll send him a photo of the page tonight."

"I'll go through that box tomorrow and see what I can make of it," I said. "For tonight, where are you gentlemen taking me to dinner?"

When I got home that evening, I went down to my lab, cast a set of wards to ensure I wasn't disturbed, and pulled the box out of the safe. I sorted the newspaper clippings, the handwritten letters, and the typed documents into separate stacks.

The letters—except for one—were in Spanish. I could read the language far better than I could speak it or understand it being spoken, but I was fifteen years out of practice. Some of the clippings were also in Spanish—from different Latin American countries—and some in English from the Washington Post. The typed documents seemed to be copies with U.S. State Department letterhead, some with FBI letterhead, and two with Office of the President letterhead. All were in English, except two in Spanish and one in German.

Two of the letters in Spanish were in Alice's hand. Two names were repeated several times in various documents and letters. Gary Akers—and the first name Gary appeared in a couple of the handwritten Spanish letters—and John Chalmers.

Gary Akers seemed familiar, but I couldn't place it. It also appeared in a yellowed newspaper clipping about a Congressional hearing into Operation Condor. I also saw Sebastian Fernandez in a short list of names in one document.

I didn't sleep well that night. Too many thoughts were spinning around in my head.

CHAPTER 31

At lunch in the Faculty Club, I saw that the special was Pacific sockeye salmon. After I finished the soup and salad I ordered, I went back to the kitchen and sweet-talked the chef into selling me two large, fresh filets.

Then I made a few phone calls before my afternoon class. They all followed the same pattern.

"Lowell, do you have any plans this evening?"

"Not specifically."

"I'm throwing a small dinner party with opening that box of Alice's for entertainment. About seven?"

"Should I bring a bottle of wine?"

"I would be pleased."

"And what are we having?"

"Poached Pacific sockeye with tarragon cream sauce, asparagus wrapped in bacon, garlic roasted new potatoes, and flan for dessert."

"I'll bring a bottle of pinot noir."

"Perfect."

I invited Lowell, Kelly, James, Steven, and David. After my class, I pedaled into town and checked on Kathleen Furman at the hospital. The nurse told me that she probably could have visitors as soon as the police cleared it. I picked up a few ingredients at the grocery store, then rode home, and put on an apron.

It was the first time I hosted more than two people since coming to Wicklow. My kitchen table was large enough to seat six, but we would have to move it and rearrange furniture in the main room. I had never tried to move the furniture, and it turned out to be much too heavy for me to do it myself. I left it until the men arrived.

One thing about academics. With our lives ordered by class schedules, most of us were used to arriving places on time. By seven o'clock, everyone was on hand, the furniture had been rearranged, and the first bottle of wine had been poured. Lowell and Steven helped me to serve the food.

"So, have you looked into our box yet?" Lowell asked as we sat to eat.

"Yes, mostly English and Spanish—a lot of Spanish—and a bit of German. A couple of names stood out, mostly due to repetition. Does the name Gary Akers mean anything to anyone?"

"Senator from Virginia," Kelly said.

"Worked for the CIA before he retired and got into politics," Lowell added. "On the Senate Intelligence Committee, I believe."

"I grew up with politics," I said. "Different politics than the U.S. government, but it left me with a preference to avoid it if I can."

"My parents live in a Virginia suburb of D.C.," Kelly said.

"Well, his name is mentioned several times. My Spanish isn't good enough to figure out if it means anything."

Steven helped me clear the table and serve the flan, coffee, and cognac. Then I plunked the box in the middle of the table and removed the cover.

"Ta-da! Sorted by type and language. And these are for notes." I handed out different colored sticky notes to each person. "Put the notes on the document."

Lowell started with the handwritten letters in Spanish, and Steven took the letter in German.

"Uh, Savanna?" Steven said a few minutes later. "This is very interesting. It's a letter from the West German government in nineteen eighty-nine. They list several men they say were East German Stasi that they think are hiding in Argentina. It's addressed to a General Jose Fernandez."

"That's Sebastian's brother," Kelly said. "His other brother is a Catholic bishop. I think Jose is in prison. When the military junta collapsed, they gave all the military and paramilitary people amnesty. But later on, they passed laws and prosecuted them."

It was almost midnight when Lowell said, "I think I have a pretty good idea why people wanted this box. Gary Akers and his supervisor John Chalmers were running a scheme in South America. They were taking cocaine the military confiscated in Bolivia and Peru, smuggling it into Los Angeles, and using the money to buy guns to outfit the paramilitaries of Operation Condor. Akers was a trainer for the death squads in Argentina and Uruguay, and Sebastian Fernandez was organizing and recruiting those paramilitary units."

He waved one of the newspaper clippings. "Both Chalmers and Akers testified before Congress that they spent little time on the ground in South America. They said they were simply liaisons with the governments down there."

"But, they could have shut Alice up years ago," I said. "Why now?"

"Akers has been mentioned as a possible presidential candidate in the next election," Kelly said.

David laughed. "I'm sure that a record of killing commies

would get him some votes, but I'm not sure running cocaine into the States would be received very well."

"How does any of this tie in to the attack on Kathleen Furman?" James asked.

"Good question." I thought about it. "I wonder if Sebastian might be getting a little nervous. If our spooks are cleaning up for Akers, anyone who knows anything might be in trouble. People like that tend not to have any loyalty to anyone but themselves."

"Especially if Akers and others think Fernandez might try to save his own neck," Lowell said. "He could get amnesty from the U.S. government by selling Akers out. Especially if the book comes out and people are looking for cover."

"So, do we tell Kagan about any of this?" I asked.

James shook his head. "Nothing we've found is of any help to Kagan. Nothing here tells us who killed Alice Henderson. I'm going back to the hotel and going to bed. I want to talk to Kathleen Furman as soon as the doctors let me in the morning."

We packed everything back into the shoebox, and James and Kelly accompanied me to my lab, where I locked it up. By the time we got back inside, I found Steven doing the dishes.

"Hey, you're a guest. You don't have to do that!"

He grinned. "A guest who wants to be invited back. I can't cook like that."

CHAPTER 32

Barclay was waiting for me when I got out of class the following day.

"Any plans for lunch?" he asked.

"Faculty Club, or sandwiches at my place," I replied.

We went to the Faculty Club.

"Did you get in to see Furman?" I asked.

"Yes. She doesn't remember much, which is understandable with a severe head injury. She said the man who was following her wore a balaclava, so no joy there. She did say it wasn't Fernandez, who—you have to admit—would stand out anywhere."

"I'm still wondering why he killed Colby. There has to be some sort of conflict between him and the spooks."

"Furman did remember her conversation with Fernandez over dinner. She had a message for him from LePage."

"Oh?"

"How much do you keep up with Council politics?"

"Not at all, if I can help it. I grew up with it, and the conflicts between my parents. Once I went away to college, I did my best to ignore all of it."

"Well, there is a faction that believes that those with power should be in charge."

"A magiocracy. Yes, that hasn't changed since the sixteen hundreds. Take all the magic users who disdain normal humans, and all the humans who hate or fear magic users, and let's have another three hundred years of war. Sounds like fun to me."

"Yes, well, LePage is one who believes magic confers higher intelligence, and so we should be in charge so we can solve all the world's problems. It fits into the right-wing fascism of Sebastian Fernandez."

"With witches taking the place of Aryan Nazis. And Kathleen Furman is part of that?"

"Evidently. She was charged with telling Fernandez he should make himself scarce. You know, move someplace like New Guinea or Tahiti and go incognito."

"Porter and his bunch should have been in favor of that. I'm really confused."

Barclay shook his head and was silent for a while. I ate my soup and half-sandwich and let him think.

"I should have a heart-to-heart with Sebastian Fernandez," he finally said.

"Not alone."

He looked surprised.

"Unless you want to end up like Jefferson Colby, I suggest you take me with you. Or are you a much stronger witch than you've led me to believe?"

"I can usually take care of myself."

"Against a life mage? Or maybe I should say a death mage? Someone who can still your heart with a rune and a word? Kelly tells me he's not a healer, but he can intervene in an animal's biological functioning. Usually, when we spot a child with that kind of magic, we give them very special training, and very special monitoring. A lot of preventative psych intervention. From what I know, that didn't happen with Dr. Fernandez."

He studied me across the table.

"And you're not afraid of that kind of magic."

"Oh, of course I am. I'm not a fool. But I can protect myself from it, and I can protect you from it."

The waiter came, and Barclay picked up the check. We walked out of the club, and I said, "He'll be in his office here right now."

With a tortured sigh, he said, "Oh, all right. Let's go see him."

Fernandez's door was closed, but I knocked. I couldn't make out what anyone was saying, but I could tell there were at least two people inside. A chair's muffle screech as it scooted across the floor. A little bit of scuffling, and then the knob turned.

"Yes?" Sebastian Fernandez asked, holding the door open just enough to look out and see Barclay standing there.

Barclay held up his identification. "Dr. Sebastian Fernandez? I'm Lieutenant James Barclay with the Pennsylvania State Police. I need to speak with you."

As he said that, he leaned against the door, slowly pushing it farther open. Fernandez was a very large man, but James was fairly big himself—young and strong.

"Well, this isn't a convenient time," Fernandez said.

I couldn't see past the two men, but James had at least some view of the inside of the office.

"I'm sure Agent Porter won't mind the interruption," James said. "As a matter of fact, I have some questions for him as well."

"Uh, well, I," Fernandez stammered as James leaned against the door a little more. Fernandez surrendered and stepped back, and James pushed the door open and stepped inside the office. I followed him.

"Uh, what is she doing here?"

"Huh?" James turned to look at me. "Oh, I find it convenient to bring a truthsayer along when I conduct these little interviews."

I was as much a truthsayer as a major league baseball player, but I kept my mouth shut.

With four of us in the office, it was a little cramped. I took a ladderback chair in the corner, and let James take the seat next to Porter, across the desk from Fernandez.

"And what did you wish to speak to me about?" Fernandez asked.

"You know a woman named Kathleen Furman, I believe? You had dinner with her a few nights ago."

"Yes. Lieutenant Kagan informed me she was later attacked. So unfortunate. We don't have that much crime in Wicklow, so it's rather shocking." Fernandez's eyes flicked toward me as he spoke. It was a bit of an effort not to smile.

"You are aware that she is a representative of a Witches' Council member in Santa Fe?"

"Yes."

"And that she is here in regard to the death of your sister-in-law, Alice Henderson."

"Former sister-in-law. That wasn't my understanding as to why she's here."

"Oh? And why is she here?"

"To protect my rights as a member of the International Council of Magical Practitioners. Lieutenant, I'm quite aware of the deranged accusations of my stepson and Tomas Ortiz. If it were up to them, I would have been hanged without a trial in Argentina when my wife died. The fact is, Pablo is unstable, and has been since he was a child. I appealed to the Council for an advocate to protect my rights, and Señorita Furman was sent here to ensure I receive the due process I am entitled to. If you're looking for her attacker, I suggest you talk to Pablo. I told Kagan that when he arrested me."

It was rare to hear the Council referred to by its full and

proper title. Barclay seemed a bit taken back by such an articulate and well-formulated speech, but he shouldn't have been. The man had an earned doctorate, and had been a professor for more than thirty years. Anyone who dealt with students on a regular basis was practiced in formulating an argument and explaining an issue.

And he was correct in citing the Council's role in a criminal or civil proceeding by the mundane authorities. I probably would have asked for a representative myself in his circumstances, but I would have asked for one who was also a lawyer—and who had some sense. But it appeared that Furman was chosen based on her ideological credentials.

"You also seem to have advocates from the U.S. government," I said, cocking my head toward Porter.

"Señor Fernandez has worked with our government in the past," Porter said. His stiff demeanor suggested that he felt insulted to be questioned by me. I wondered if the broomstick up his butt was placed there before or after he was hired by the CIA.

"We're aware of Operation Condor," I said, "as well as the arrest warrant issued in Argentina."

Fernandez erupted in a profanity-laced tirade against the "Communists who hold my country in thrall," and the "lies and insinuations" against him. He turned very red in the face, mixing English and Spanish, and slamming his fist on the desk. I slipped my hand up my sleeve and gripped my wand, unsure if he was still in control of himself. It was rather enlightening to compare his temper with that of Pablo Arias.

He finished with, "Out! Get out! I don't have to listen to this!"

Barclay calmly said, "I'm not particularly interested in your political beliefs. I am interested as to where you gentlemen were at the time Ms. Furman was attacked. If you would be so kind as to tell me where you went after your dinner with her."

"He came by my hotel, and I gave him a ride home," Porter said.

"You took him directly home? What time was this?"

Porter narrowed his eyes. "I don't think I have to submit to your interrogation."

With a bit of a smile, Barclay pulled out his police ID and said, "Mr. Porter, you can answer my questions here, or we can go down to the police station, call your lawyer, and answer them there."

Porter pulled out his ID. "I'm here in my official capacity. I suggest you speak with my superiors if you want to interview me." The condescending smile on his face told me that he considered himself untouchable. But he had been dealing with Sam Kagan too long, and Barclay wasn't impressed.

Barclay sighed. "Keith Porter, you're under arrest for obstruction of a police investigation." He stood and went on to read Porter his rights. "Please stand."

Porter exploded out of his chair, facing Barclay and screaming, "You bloody idiot! You can't arrest me!"

"Ne quoquam exsurgatis!"

I cast a spell to restrict Porter's movement. Barclay handcuffed him.

"Ut eras." I uttered, allowing Barclay to pull the man to the door.

"What the hell? You can't do this. I'm an officer of the United States Government."

"Mr. Porter," Barclay said, "you have no official capacity here. As far as I'm concerned, you're just a potential criminal."

"You'll pay for this. You'll be lucky to work as a street sweeper."

Porter was getting on my nerves, so I muttered, *"Silentium,"* and he shut up.

"Thrift store magic," Fernandez sneered at me.

I grinned at him. "*Alegrate no estoy enjado contigo,*" I said in Spanish. Be glad I'm not angry at you.

Barclay hauled Porter out of the office, and I followed. He turned back and said, "I'm not finished, Dr. Fernandez. I have more questions."

Barclay dragged Porter down the hall, but in the wrong direction.

"Where are you taking him?" I asked.

"To the campus police. They have a couple of cells there, and they're true null-magic containment cells. I think Chief Crumley has more experience with unreasonable magic users than the local police."

CHAPTER 33

"Do you really think you can hold him?" I asked after Barclay and Alistair Crumley locked Porter in a cell.

"I'm interested in what kind of reasoning his superiors are going to use to try and get him out," Barclay answered.

Crumley chuckled. "I've called Santa Fe. Councilor Robinson is sending us a lawyer."

"How many agents does Porter have here in Wicklow?" I asked.

"Three, I believe," Barclay said. "We'll find out for sure after we give him his phone call."

Porter did call someone, and then told us that his lawyer would be in Wicklow the following afternoon, which would be Friday. The lawyer my father promised was due to land in Pittsburgh shortly before noon, and Crumley said he would send his second-in-command to pick him up.

"Well, it will be Monday before we can arraign him and his buddies can bail him out," Barclay said when we finally left the campus police office. "What is there to do in Wicklow over the weekend?"

I laughed.

"I understand the fishing is good, although it's forecast to be a little cold. The river doesn't freeze over, however. Kelly could tell you about the cross-country skiing. I haven't checked as to what's showing at the movie theater. It has two screens, and they change the movies every week. There are a lot of sports bars."

"And what do you do on the weekends?" he asked.

"I read, watch Netflix, occasionally have dinner with friends. Prepare materials for labs or work on lectures. Some weekends I grade papers, but I don't have any of that right now. I save most of my exciting activities for the breaks between trimesters."

He grinned. "And what do you do on your breaks?"

"Travel, mostly. I'm considering New Zealand for this winter, and then Spain for spring break, and France next summer. Wicklow operates on ten-week trimesters. Most of our students are well-off, so the philosophy here is that opportunities for travel and extended learning are educational. In practice, I think most of them just party, although partying in places such as Prague and St. Petersburg can be very educational. As to the faculty, I think we need longer breaks than those who are teaching at normal colleges. I'm constantly on edge hoping no one blows anything up."

"And you'll be traveling alone?"

"Unless I find someone congenial who would like to accompany me," I said with a smile.

"I've never been to New Zealand," he said, and smiled back at me. "Well, I'm hungry. What about tonight? Lowell and Susan's place?"

I shook my head. "I don't think so. That's twice I've been attacked on that road. Let's do something in town."

We stopped by my apartment so I could drop off some stuff and change clothes. I glanced out the window facing the street and saw one of Porter's goons watching from across the street.

"Where is your car parked?"

"Over by the library. Why?"

"Because we have company across the street."

He came over and peeked through the window.

"Any other way out of here?"

I motioned to the door to the garden. "Yes. We can go through my lab or the greenhouse, then through a graduate student dorm to the Quad."

"Let's do that," he said. "Just to inconvenience them a little."

We drove downtown to the European bistro.

"I suggest that you park behind Lowell's bookstore," I said. "Porter's frat boys knifed Steven's tires the last time he was down here with me."

"You're joking."

"I wish I was. I'm not sure what criteria the CIA uses to recruit their agents, but they don't seem to place a premium on intelligence. The Central Idiots Agency?"

I told him about my dinner with Kathleen and its aftermath while we walked to the bistro.

"Assuming we made a clean getaway from the College, we might make it through the evening without my normal shadows, but I wouldn't bet on it," I said. "With Porter out of commission, his men don't have any direction, so I would expect them to fall back on familiar patterns."

"For someone who was a forensic accountant, or whatever your cover was with the Council, you seem to know a lot about clandestine activities," Barclay remarked.

"Don't speculate down that dark alley too far," I replied. "I'd hate to have to kill you."

His expression was a little alarming, so I smiled and winked. "When I moved here, Kelly told me I'd be reading a lot. She and I trade mysteries and thrillers, and Lowell has a room in the back where he sells used books, so it makes it affordable."

He didn't really look as though he believed me, but I

laughed again and took his arm. I didn't see any of the CIA guys during the two blocks between Lowell's and the bistro. When we arrived, we discovered that either Thursdays were a hot night for eating out in Wicklow, or that the sauerbraten special was a Wicklow favorite. Whatever the case, we had to wait for half an hour at their little wine bar before they seated us.

"I think I'll have the special," I said, even before opening the menu.

James watched a waitress walk by with four servings of the German specialty on a tray.

"Yeah. I think we should order before they run out."

"We won't run out," a voice said. I looked up to find a waitress standing next to our table, holding a pitcher of water. "Thursdays is German night, with either sauerbraten, rouladen, or bratwurst and sauerkraut. We rotate it."

"Oh. And what night is French night?"

She grinned. "Wednesday. You just missed it."

We ordered the special and a bottle of wine.

I had mostly ordered French or Spanish dishes when eating there, but discovered their German recipes to be as tasty as anything I had eaten in Germany. By the time we finished splitting a baked apple for dessert, accompanied by shots of Jägermeister and espresso, I was ready for a wheelbarrow to cart me out of the place.

Then we walked outside to find all three of Porter's flunkeys standing around waiting for us. One directly across the street, between us and James's car, one across the street to our right, and the third leaning on a tree half a block down the street to our left.

"My, how thoughtful of them to provide us with an escort," I said. "You know, we could duck into the sports bar next door and let them freeze out here."

"I wonder which one of us is carrying a tracking spell," James said.

"Now, that is a question for a suspicious mind. You know, if I were alone, I might call Sam Kagan and tell him I'm being stalked. But surely, they wouldn't harass a State Police officer, would they?"

"I'm not taking any bets with these guys. Let's go hit that sports bar and we'll give Kagan a call. If nothing else, he gives us a witness if we have to kill someone."

I wasn't sure I was comfortable with going that far, but avoiding a confrontation was at the top of my list for the evening. We turned and walked toward the bar. I didn't check to see if any of our stalkers followed us until we reached the bar and James held the door open for me. Sure enough, at least one of them was still with us.

We found a couple of stools at the bar, and James called Kagan. It was a little too noisy even to hear James's side of the conversation, but he seemed pleased when he put his phone away.

"He said he'd stop by with a squad car and give us a ride home. I think he wants to hear firsthand from me as to why I arrested Porter."

CHAPTER 34

Every time I left my apartment that weekend, at least one of the CIA guys followed me. And on Sunday, I thought I saw a new one.

Arthur Ballinger, my father's lawyer, came in from Denver on Saturday. I thought it was interesting that he'd booked a room at Carragher's Retreat instead of the Grand Hotel in Wickford. James denied any involvement with that, and when I spoke to my father, he said Chief Crumley recommended it.

Porter's lawyer, Peter Hawley, also came in and took a room at the Grand. My father filled me in on his background.

"A graduate of Wicklow," Dad said, "and Harvard Law. Worked for the State Department for a while, went into private practice, then took an appointment with the CIA. Specializes in international law. One of the judges in Wicklow went to the college there at the same time. His stints with the government have been very profitable. His parents were well off, but he's become a millionaire working for the CIA."

"What about his magic?" I asked.

"Persuasion—no one has ever accused him of coercion as far as I know—along with aeromancy and illusion. Did I mention that he worked in South America when he was with the State Department?"

Hawley met with his client on Sunday morning, then with James and Ballinger that afternoon. I wasn't allowed to be a fly on the wall, but James told me later that Hawley had shut down any questioning.

"He's planning on filing a motion at the arraignment that since his client has committed no crime, and because I'm bullying him, they should just let him go," James said. He laughed. "They even dragged out the idea of suing me for police brutality. I offered to bring in a photographer to document the bruises, and they backed down."

"Maybe this is a good time to interview Fernandez."

"If I can find him. He met with Hawley on Saturday evening, and then vanished. His car is gone as well."

"Any chance he skipped town?"

"If I were a betting man, I'd put a hundred down."

※

Porter was arraigned on Monday morning. The State prosecutor asked that his passport be confiscated, and identified him as a flight risk. Hawley tried to get the charges dismissed, but the judge, unimpressed by a fancy lawyer from Washington, informed him that was what trials were for.

That evening, James picked me and Kelly up and took us out to Carragher's for dinner with Ballinger.

Susan escorted us to a cozy private dining room and shut the door. Arthur Ballenger and Lowell Carragher were already there.

"Savanna. So lovely to see you again. It's been ages," Ballenger said, standing as we came in.

"Mr. Ballenger. I think the last time was at my graduation."

The graduation for my bachelor's degree. It had been twenty years.

He chuckled. "Has it been that long? I guess you've been behaving yourself."

"I haven't needed your services, so either I've behaved myself or I haven't been caught."

He laughed out loud.

"I guess I should have suspected you knew each other," James said as we seated ourselves.

"I used to call him Uncle Arthur, but I'm afraid people would think that was unprofessional, as well as make him feel old. It was probably more fitting when I was twelve years old."

"I've been Lead Counsel to the Witches' Council for almost thirty years," Ballenger said. "Savanna often was my gracious hostess when I stayed at her father's place in Santa Fe. I must say, I've missed your cooking since you went away to college. Not that your stepmother is a bad cook, but you have a special way with food."

Lowell poured wine for us. We weren't presented with any menus, which tipped me off that a fresh walleye dinner was in my future. Ballenger didn't waste any time, asking questions that started with the status of the Wicklow murders as of the day he arrived, and working backward.

"We're brainstorming here," he said at one point. "Can anyone think of a single reason why someone would kill Jefferson Colby?"

No one answered, although many of us shook our heads.

"He was a major asshole," I said, "but Porter is an even bigger one. I would cheerfully direct any of the CIA jerks to take a long walk off a short pier."

"What stumps me," Kelly said, "is why he chose my side yard to die. I mean, I'm positive that was Sebastian Fernandez's footprint in my flowerbed, but why would he kill Colby?" She chuckled. "It's funny, but since that night, I check men's feet when I meet them. So far, no one has a foot that large except Fernandez. And maybe Pablo. That man looks like he's wearing clown shoes."

I realized that I had never looked at Pablo's feet. In spite of his pudgy build, his trousers always looked baggy and sort of puddled at the cuffs.

"So," Ballenger said, "we have the mystery of who killed Alice Henderson, and even the bigger mysteries as to who wanted Jefferson Colby and Kathleen Furman dead. And no one can figure out the connection between the three?"

"Gary Akers?" I ventured.

"And his old friend Marcus LePage," Ballenger said. "Yes, that is the obvious answer, with Sebastian Fernandez tying the package together."

"You don't sound convinced," Barclay said.

We were interrupted by a waiter and a waitress who brought in a huge grilled walleye on a platter, along with bowls of green beans, potatoes, and gravy. Lowell did the honors of serving the fish while we passed the side dishes family style.

When everyone was served and had a chance to taste their meals, Ballenger said, "Everything fits together and makes sense. Our only problem is that there isn't a shred of evidence. As far as the CIA, I don't think there is any chance we can tie them being here to Akers. It just ain't gonna happen. We can tie Akers to Fernandez, but only if we can bust Fernandez for something. Otherwise, we have no justification for dredging up his Operation Condor days."

We were almost finished with our meals, when Barclay got a phone call. He excused himself and left the room, but was back less than five minutes later.

"That was Sam Kagan," he announced. "A State Policeman just reported Sebastian Fernandez's car off the road in the Allegheny River about twenty miles south of Wicklow. I need to go."

"Do you want some company?" I asked.

He shook his head. "No, one of my men reported it. At the moment, it's a routine traffic accident, and I'll call when I know something."

I followed him out anyway.

"Are you okay to drive?" I asked. "We've put away several bottles of wine."

That stopped him, and I could tell he was trying to gauge his state of sobriety.

"Crap. Probably not the best idea."

"Ask Susan to fix you some coffee to go. And drink this." I handed him a small bottle with brown liquid. "You'll pay for it tomorrow, though."

He looked at the bottle, pulled out the stopper, and sucked it down. Then he leaned toward me and kissed me on the cheek.

"Thanks, Savanna."

He walked over to Susan, spoke to her, then waited by the front door until she came back with a takeout cup and handed it to him.

Susan's son drove Kelly and me back to town. I thought it was rather cute the way he seemed to jump at the chance, and how he kept glancing at her all the way into town. She was ten years older than he was, but the boy was obviously infatuated. Kelly pretended not to notice, but she was nice to him.

CHAPTER 35

Barclay called the following morning, but it wasn't early. The potion I gave him the night before alleviated the immediate effects of the alcohol but added to the residual effects. The result was a doubling of the hangover symptoms.

"We found Fernandez's Mercedes halfway in the river, with the driver's side door open. No sign of him or anyone else, but there were tracks and drag marks on the bank."

"No idea how the car went off the road?" I asked.

"Skid marks, then down the embankment. The officer who found it said he's seen two other vehicles go over in that same spot. I could see that someone not paying attention and going too fast might have a problem with that curve."

"But no driver."

"Nope."

"What do you mean, drag marks?"

"Like someone dragged something heavy up the bank from the car."

"Like a body?"

"Possibly. You don't happen to have a hangover potion, do you?"

I laughed. "I told you there'd be consequences in the morning. Where are you?"

"At the hotel."

"Come by and I'll fix you breakfast."

It was always a bad idea to use magic to fix one ailment then apply more magic to fix the results. I figured a good breakfast would help. A breakfast smoothie made with frozen mango and fresh strawberries, along with a poached egg over avocado toast and a side of crunchy, sliced red bell peppers would do the trick.

James showed up about the time I had it all ready.

After we ate, he said, "How come you aren't married?"

I laughed. "Too intimidating and too picky. I took a boy I was dating in college home to meet my mother. He lasted two days of what was supposed to be a week-long holiday. You know what they say, Lieutenant, if you want to see what your future wife will look like in thirty years, look at her mother."

"And nobody since then?"

"Oh, I haven't taken a nun's vows. I've had a few relationships, but marriage is a universe I haven't been tempted to explore."

Kelly called a little while later.

"I just got a call from Señor Ortiz," she said. "He's worried that Pablo hasn't been at the hotel for the past two days. Have you seen James?"

"He's right here." I handed the phone to him. "It's Kelly."

I cleared the dishes from the table, took them to the kitchen, and put on the kettle for some tea. When I finished, James handed me my phone.

"According to Ortiz, he hasn't seen Pablo Arias in two days. His sister is worried. So, we have two men who hate each other and both are missing. If they killed each other, I hope they did it someplace we'll find the bodies so I can close this case."

"So, you think that one of them killed Alice?"

He rolled his eyes. "I don't know what I think." With a deep sigh, he heaved himself out of his chair.

"I guess I should go talk to Ortiz. Want to come along?"

I told him I had classes to teach but asked him to call, and he made his way out the door. I got dressed to go to work.

I was distracted during my morning classes. Hoping James would show up when I broke for lunch, I was disappointed. I called Kelly, and we agreed to meet for lunch at the Faculty Club.

"You haven't heard anything?" she asked after we gave our orders to the waiter.

"Not since you spoke to him this morning. He said he was going to talk to Señor Ortiz."

"And nothing about Fernandez's car?"

I shook my head. "I spoke with Katy Bosun, and she said that Carver told her to cancel his classes, but she doesn't have a clue of what's going on."

That was fairly shocking since Katy, Dean Carver's secretary, usually knew more than God about what was going on at Wicklow College.

That afternoon, I had a tutorial at my lab next to my apartment. Again, I was rather distracted, but with graduate students, I could direct them to take the lead in a subject of interest. As a result, we wandered off into some of the more esoteric techniques for brewing and distilling potions, and I only had to keep them from falling into the major rabbit holes. I was woolgathering, wondering why Pablo would disappear, when one student's rather forceful statement brought me back to the conversation.

"Wait a minute!" I said rather loudly, focusing all their attention on me. "Yes, I know that you can do a fast alcohol distillation of that particular set of botanicals. But when you pour the two products together, you had better have a good exhaust hood, breathing masks, gloves, and eye protection. Your margin of error at stage three is about two or three degrees Celsius. Screwing it up will not only produce an explosion but also poison anyone unprotected in the lab, or within twenty meters of the lab if you have a leak."

I had their attention, especially that of the student who had been advocating that particular shortcut.

"As with a number of other things, just because you can do something, doesn't mean you should. A two-week infusion of the herbs in alcohol will produce a potion that is ninety percent as potent, but without the risk. Here, let me show you the proper spells to cast at each stage of the process."

I took a deep breath and reminded myself that I was teaching alchemy, not English literature, and focused on seven very bright, and potentially very dangerous, students.

An hour later, after showing the students out the door, I checked my phone. I had a message from Kelly, one from James, and one from Tomas Ortiz. All of them wanted me to go to the Wayfarer Inn. I dumped my books and briefcase at my apartment, hurriedly changed clothes, and jumped on my bike.

CHAPTER 36

Kelly was waiting on a bench outside the restaurant at the Wayfarer Inn when I rode up. I chained my bicycle to the bench and sat down beside her.

"What's up?"

James came out of the hotel and said, "We found Pablo's rental car. It was parked downtown and had half a dozen parking tickets on it, dating back three days."

"So, where do two men wander off to, without their cars, in Wicklow in November?"

Kelly and James both shook their heads.

The waitress who had told me about the row between Pablo and Kathleen Furman came out of the restaurant, nodded to us, then walked over to a large ashtray past my bike and lit a cigarette.

"You haven't seen the Argentinian guy lately, have you?" I asked the woman.

She shrugged. "Not for a couple of days, but that's not unusual. Sometimes he disappears for a couple of weeks without checking out. Sort of a strange one."

"A couple of weeks?" Kelly asked.

"Yeah. Last summer he kind of came and went, almost like he lived here. And then when that woman died up at the College, he drove off that afternoon, and didn't show up again until he came back with his sister. That was at least a couple of weeks, and he never checked out. We get a lot of salesmen who are in and out, but they check in and out. That guy should rent a house here in town. It would be cheaper."

"You're saying that he was in town when that woman fell out of the window?" I asked.

"Yeah. I ran into him as I was coming on shift, and he was in a major rush. Came out the door with a suitcase and almost knocked me down. Jumped in his car—I think it was a rental car, he seems to change cars a lot—and drove out of here like his tail was on fire. That evening, one of the local cops came in on his break and told us about the accident up at the College."

Kelly and I looked at each other. The waitress finished her cigarette and went back inside.

"I thought the first time Pablo was here was when he came with Maria," James said.

"So did I," Kelly said.

"Why did you want to see me?" I asked.

He looked around, almost as though checking to see if anyone was listening.

"I have a search warrant for Sebastian Fernandez's house, but I would prefer not to have to break the door down. I have it on excellent authority that you're the best cat burglar in town. Can you do a lock for me?"

I glared at Kelly, who did her best to put on an innocent expression and not laugh.

"As long as you have a warrant. Or, I could teach you the spell." I grinned at him. "It could come in handy the next time you have a warrant and don't want to break anything."

"That sounds like an excellent idea." He glanced at my bike. "Perhaps we should take my car?"

Sebastian Fernandez's house was about a mile from the college, and a mile from the Wayfarer Inn. I was glad I didn't have to ride there, as the road was rather steep. James drove up the hill, then turned onto a side street. Shortly thereafter, he turned again into a long driveway. When we finally reached the house, we saw a car parked in front.

"That's not one of Dr. Fernandez's cars," Kelly said. "He thinks American cars are crap."

James parked, picked up the microphone of his police radio, and asked for a check on the license plate. After a couple of minutes, the dispatcher came back and said the car was registered to a rental company in Youngstown, Ohio.

We got out, and I walked to the front door with James.

"Well, I guess you won't need my services," I said.

The door—which was solid oak and two inches thick—looked as though it had been kicked in.

"Either a hydraulic ram or magic," he said, drawing his pistol, "even Godzilla couldn't kick that door in. Stay back."

I drew my wand and let him slowly push the door open. I followed him into the foyer but stayed several feet behind him. The house was large, all on one floor, and fairly modern inside. Kelly had said Fernandez employed a housekeeper, and from what I could see, she did a good job.

Barclay cautiously checked each room as he came to it, then we heard a noise from the back of the house off to our right. He moved in that direction, taking care to make no noise.

He turned a corner into a room and shouted, "Freeze! Police!"

I heard a crash, and Barclay ducked back out of the room. Some sort of debris showered around him. That was followed by the sound of breaking glass. I chanced a look around the corner and saw someone disappear through a broken window.

I ran to the window and cast a spell, "*Ne quoquam exsurgatis!*"

I was late, and knew it. The back of the man's coat disappeared into the woods. I turned back to James. He leaned against the door jamb, with the remains of a shattered desk lamp on the floor around him.

"Are you okay?"

"Yeah, I think so." He turned his face toward me. There was a small cut on the side of his forehead above his left eye.

"You'll live," I said. "Pablo?"

"Yeah. He got away?"

"I was too slow."

I looked around the room. In contrast to the immaculate state of the other rooms we had passed through, the office—which I guessed it was—had been torn apart. Pablo was looking for something, but no telling if he'd found it or not.

"I'm going to check on Kelly," I said, and rushed out of the house.

I found her crouched behind James's car with her wand in hand.

"You guys all right in there?" she called. "I heard something break."

"Did you see Pablo?" I called back. James's car was parked behind the rental, so he couldn't have driven away.

"Nope. He was in there?"

"Yes, but he escaped into the woods."

She shrugged. "It's not that far back into town."

James came out of the house and made a call on his radio. When he finished, he told us, "I called Kagan to have forensics take fingerprints in that room, and have the car checked." He sighed. "Well, at least we know one of our missing men is still alive."

CHAPTER 37

Sam Kagan showed up with a couple of uniformed cops in a squad car, and a forensics van following them.

"I put out an APB for Pablo," he told Barclay, "and I brought a boot for that rental car. We checked, and it is rented to him. We also booted the rental car we found in town."

The boot he was talking about was a so-called Denver boot, which went over a wheel and disabled the car.

One of the first things they did was break into the trunk of the rental car. The look of relief on Barclay's face told me that he'd been afraid Fernandez's body might be there, but the space was empty.

"No traces of blood, Lieutenant," a forensics guy said. "We didn't find anything inside the car, either."

"Where is he going to go?" Kelly asked. "It's too cold at night to stay outside."

I thought about it. "You should probably put a man on Alice's apartment. I'm willing to bet he has a key."

"Isn't it warded?" Barclay asked, looking to Kagan.

"I don't think so," the other cop answered. "I didn't ward it, anyway. I'll send a man over there."

One of the forensics officers searching the car called, "Lieutenant? You should see this."

Kagan walked over and looked at a small box in the glove compartment.

"Wonderful," he said, then went to his car, and got on the radio.

Barclay went to look in the glove compartment, then came back to where Kelly and I were watching the festivities.

"Box of .38 caliber bullets," Barclay said. "Pablo has a gun."

"You should also put a man—or maybe a policewoman—on Maria," Kelly said. "They have separate rooms at the hotel. If anyone can talk him into giving himself up, it's her."

He walked over to Kagan and they had a long talk. When he came back, he said, "Sam's put out an all-points bulletin on both Pablo and Fernandez. I think we have to corral them and get to the bottom of some things."

"Have they found anything in Fernandez's house?" I asked. "That looked like his private office that Pablo was tearing apart."

Barclay shook his head. "He wasn't carrying anything when he went out that window, and Kagan's people haven't found anything linking Fernandez to Alice Henderson."

"You know, I've been thinking. Could Fernandez run off the road because of an illusion?"

"Possible. I thought Pablo was a conjurer. No one said anything about illusions."

"Who knows what he might conjure. Certainly not a demon out on that open road without the ritualistic trappings, but perhaps something else? I'm not really up on conjuration."

"Me neither, but I can have someone check. Or maybe he has hidden talents."

"Unless one of his hidden talents keeps him warm, he has to find someplace to spend the night," I said, looking up at the heavy cloud cover. "Forecast is for rain tonight, and it will be cold."

He nodded, then walked over to Kagan, and they talked some more. It was growing dark. Barclay signaled for Kelly and me to get in the car, and we drove back to town.

"The sheriff's office and state police are going to check places out of town. A lot of farms around here and seasonal vacation cabins," James said. "Kelly, do you think he could get violent with strangers? I mean, would he break into people's houses? Take hostages?"

Kelly laughed. "I don't think that's something he wants to try around here. You might not have noticed, but there is a lot of fresh venison and wild turkey on tables in Western Pennsylvania right now. Add in the fact that probably half the farmers in the county have some kind of magic, and they're likely to be unimpressed by his pistol."

Barclay nodded. "Pretty much like everywhere between Philadelphia and Pittsburgh."

"There are probably more witches in this county than in the Pittsburgh metro area, with forty times the population," she said. "Wicklow is special."

He chuckled. "I agree with that. My mother's parents live about thirty miles northwest of here. My granddad might shoot him, but I'd be more afraid of my grandmother's magic."

We swung by Lowell's bookstore and asked if he would come along to talk to Maria. He closed the shop but took his own car to the hotel. Once we arrived, we invited Tomas and Maria to a conference room the hotel made available to the police.

"Pablo is in trouble," Barclay started, with Lowell translating for Maria. "He broke into Sebastian Fernandez's home, caused some damage, assaulted a police officer, and we think he has a pistol. We also found Dr. Fernandez's car run off the road. He can help himself by turning himself in. The major thing is he does not need to get himself into more trouble. Can you contact him?"

Both Lowell and Señor Ortiz spoke with Maria, and the conversation went on for at least ten minutes. I could follow a little bit of it—enough to know that she didn't know where Pablo was, she didn't think he would listen to her, and it was the police's fault for not already arresting Fernandez.

They seemed to come to a conclusion, and Lowell said, "She will call him, and try to talk him into surrendering. Tomas agrees it's the best solution."

She took her phone out to the hall and called while the rest of us waited. After a few minutes, she came back and spoke to Tomas. Lowell was close enough to follow their conversation. Finally, Tomas spoke in English to the rest of us.

"She says that Pablo has Sebastian, who confessed to Camila's death." The old man held up his hand and shrugged. "Yes, I know such a confession won't hold up in a court of law. Anyway, he is at a cabin near where you found Sebastian's car. She didn't get an address from him."

It was Barclay's turn to go out into the hall and make a phone call. When he came back, he thanked Maria and Tomas, then we left the hotel.

CHAPTER 38

James swung by Kelly's house and dropped her off, then took me to the college. We were almost there when his police radio squawked.

"Lieutenant, the city police sent a message that they've found Pablo Arias." The dispatcher went on to provide directions and GPS coordinates. I watched them appear on the electronic map on the dashboard.

"Do you want me to drop you off?" James asked.

"I'm fine. Let's go see what the young man is up to."

We drove on south out of town. About fifteen minutes after we passed the College, we rounded a corner, and James said, "That's where we found the Mercedes."

There was a gap in the guardrail, with the river on the other side.

He soon slowed the car, and then braked and turned left onto a narrow dirt road. It was a bit muddy due to the recent snow and the rain that was starting to fall. I could see the tracks of more cars.

Another turnoff led to a small meadow where six different cop cars—Wicklow City, State of Pennsylvania, County Sheriff, and Sam Kagan's unmarked car—were parked. There was also an ambulance. James pulled in with the rest of them. Kagan jumped out of his car and ran over, getting in the back of James's car.

"The cabin is just on top of that rise," he said. "Belongs to a couple from Chicago who come out here in the summers. We contacted them, and they gave us the code to the electronic locks on the doors. Said the only heat is a small woodstove, and they have the water turned off, but someone could easily turn it back on. Private well. There are lights on in the house, and the officers staking the place out say they've seen someone moving around inside."

I couldn't see the house from where I sat, but I could see what looked like a thin plume of smoke rising ahead of us.

"Is there a phone in the house?" James asked.

"No. Do you have Pablo's cell phone?"

"Yeah, I have it," I said.

"So do I," James said. "Has anyone contacted him at all? Does he know we're out here?"

Kagan shook his head. "You said his sister told you where he is. I think we're probably expected."

With a sigh, James unbuckled his seatbelt. "I guess I should go up there and call him. Sam, if you could hand me that coat in the back seat."

"You have a vest?" Kagan asked as he handed James the coat.

"Yeah, it's in the trunk."

He got out of the car, opened the trunk, and I watched as he strapped on a bulletproof vest. He came back to the front of the car and pulled on his coat over it.

I pulled my wand out of my sleeve, drew a rune, and cast a spell. Then I got out of the car.

"Hey, where are you going?" Kagan asked.

"I can't see anything from here," I answered.

"You can't go up there," he said. "You're a civilian. You could get shot."

I grinned at him. "I'm not getting wet. I'm willing to bet I won't get shot, either."

James eyed me. "Nice spell."

"One of my favorites. Shall we go?"

We trudged up the muddy road for a hundred feet or so and came to a flat area. The road ended there, and a large log cabin sat at the back of the cleared area. Smoke from a stovepipe above the roof could be clearly seen, and about half the windows showed light behind them.

James moved over under a tree, where a couple of state cops were huddled trying to stay dry. He pulled out his phone and called.

"Pablo? This is Lieutenant James Barclay with the State Police. I think your sister told you we would be coming? If you please come out, unarmed, with your hands up, I think we can peacefully resolve this situation."

I couldn't hear the other side of the conversation, but James listened for a while.

"Yes, I'm willing to listen to what you have to say, and I am aware of an arrest warrant outstanding for Dr. Fernandez in Argentina," James said.

He was silent, listening, for a few more minutes.

"All right. Come on out. Unarmed, Mr. Arias. Do you understand?"

He put his phone away, shaking his head. "I'm not sure if he's coming out or not."

We stood there for several minutes, then I got impatient and slipped away. Everyone's attention was on the house, and they didn't even turn their heads when I left. I circled around to the side of the place, noticing the police on guard on that side.

Even if there had been a moon, the clouds would have

hidden it. With the rain and the dense forest all around, I could barely see my hand, and I couldn't hear anything but the rain. A porch wrapped all the way around the house, and the eaves of the roof hung over it. I stepped onto the porch and saw movement from the corner of my eye. The cops on that side of the house saw me for the first time.

I snuck around, peeking in the windows, and found Fernandez, sitting in a chair by the kitchen table. He was restrained with duct tape to the chair. He wasn't muzzled, and I could see a bruise on the side of his head.

Pablo came in from another room and tossed a cell phone on the table. He said something, but I couldn't hear it. I thought Fernandez might have said something in return. Then Pablo turned and left the room.

I snuck back along the porch to the back of the house. A quick check revealed that the code we'd been given worked on the back door. I heard a click when it unlocked, but I didn't try to open the door. Instead, I left the porch and walked to where the cops in the back of the house were watching from under a tree. I fished around in the pocket of my coat and found my phone.

"Barclay," James said when he answered.

"Staying dry?"

"Where the hell are you?"

"Sitting under a big tree, hoping we don't get a lightning strike, with a couple of cute young state troopers, or whatever you call them here. You and Sam were being boring. Sebastian is in the room with the light on facing you farthest to your right. Pablo is pacing back and forth between that room and the one in the front. What do you plan to do? Sit here all night in the rain?"

CHAPTER 39

Barclay made his way over to where I waited. It was pretty boring sitting under a tree in the rain watching the house. The state cops had a thermos of coffee and an extra cup—one of those folding cups—and they shared. That was nice. The shield spell kept me dry, but the damp cold seeped through the shield and coat.

"Anything happening?" Barclay asked.

"The house is just sitting there," I said. "Do you want me to shake it and see if it's still awake?"

The uniform cops laughed, but Barclay didn't.

"I checked that door code and unlocked the back door, but I didn't try to go in. Fernandez is taped to a chair in that room." I pointed.

"Is that shield of yours really bulletproof?" he asked.

"Yeah. It's even student-proof."

He studied the house, then said, "And the back door is unlocked? So, we could go in the back when you knock on the front door."

"Sure. Then you can shoot it out with Fernandez in the middle. Sounds like a plan to me."

He glared at me.

"James, I don't know how you're going to protect Fernandez. I assume that he's drugged or unconscious. His magic doesn't require the use of his hands or mouth, and Pablo's still upright. I don't want him shot, either."

"Can you contain him?"

"Perhaps. Perhaps we can have a mage battle in the sitting room and destroy the house. I don't truly know his magic, or his strength. Can you try and call him again and see if he'll give up?"

He gave me an exasperated look, but pulled out his phone, and hit redial.

It seemed to ring and ring, then I saw Pablo cross the window in the room where he was holding Fernandez. I was close enough to James that I could hear Pablo's voice over the phone.

"What?"

"Are you coming out?" James asked. "Or do you plan to spend the winter in that cabin? You know that little woodstove is the only heat, don't you?"

"Are you going to arrest this sorry bastard?"

"I'm going to arrest both of you so that I can sort this mess out. What do you expect me to do?"

I wasn't sure that was the best way to approach the matter, even if it was the truth.

"I have his confession recorded," Pablo said. "He killed my mother. He stole my life, my sister's life. He has hundreds of deaths on his hands."

"Yes, and there is a warrant for his arrest in Argentina," James said. "Pablo, you have to let the law handle this."

"I've been waiting thirty years for the law to handle it. And nothing! Nothing!" Pablo was shouting loud enough that even the troopers, ten feet away, could hear him.

"Pablo, I'm going to send Dr. Robinson into the house. I need to make sure Dr. Fernandez is all right."

I saw Pablo come to the window and look out, then disappear again.

"Let Dr. Robinson in. If you give her the gun, and allow her to check Dr. Fernandez, we can settle this tonight. All right?"

"Okay, send her in," Pablo said. "I won't hurt her."

James hung up.

"Why in the hell are you sending me in there? What if he doesn't keep his word? What if I have to hurt him? I don't like this, James."

"You notice what he left out?"

"Of course. He didn't say that Fernandez killed Alice."

"And I need that confession."

I mumbled some very unladylike things, tucked my wand back into my sleeve, then stood and headed toward the cabin. As I crossed the space between the large tree and the front door, I saw the two state cops start to circle around toward the back door.

When I reached the porch, I set my phone to record, dropped it back into my coat pocket, then knocked on the door. I stood there, feeling like a fool, trying to figure out how I got talked into confronting a murderer with a gun. Didn't my mother raise me to be a little smarter than that? I could just imagine her shaking her head in sorrow.

The door opened, and Pablo looked beyond me. He was holding a pistol in his hand, but not pointing it at me.

"You're alone?"

"Yes." I held out my hands. "And unarmed."

He pushed the screen door open with his foot. I walked through into the house. The first thing I noticed was that it wasn't much warmer inside than on the porch, although it was dryer. I assumed there might be bedding in the house, but it didn't promise to be a comfortable place to spend the night.

"Where is Dr. Fernandez?" I asked.

He stood aside and pointed with the pistol. "In there."

As I had seen through the window, Fernandez was sitting in one of the chairs surrounding the kitchen table—a chair far too small for the man's large frame. Pablo had used duct tape to bind his legs to the chair legs, bind his hands together behind his back, and wrap his torso to the chair back. I couldn't see how he could have done that with Fernandez being awake. But I guessed that he had been unconscious. He appeared barely awake as I studied him.

His face was a mass of bruises, and I was fairly certain his nose was broken. I assumed his body, under his clothes, would show more bruising. I wondered how Pablo had originally subdued him.

"Dr. Fernandez? Are you all right?" I asked.

He tried to open his swollen eyes to look at me. "*No bueno.*"

I felt a whisper of magic but couldn't readily identify it. Pablo was trying to do something, but it was not a common spell that I recognized.

Fernandez screamed, and I suddenly knew what was going on. Pablo might be a conjurer as I'd been told, but he definitely had the power of life magic—the malicious control of a living entity's life processes. The type of magic Kelly told me Fernandez controlled, but obviously Pablo was stronger. Whether he was strong enough to penetrate my shield, I didn't know.

I spun around, drawing my wand from my sleeve. "*Gravis ferre!*"

Pablo dropped the pistol, its weight suddenly too much to lift.

"*Ne quoquam exsurgatis!*"

Pablo laughed. "You can spell the gun, but you can't spell me. I control life."

"But you couldn't fix your aunt's cancer."

He shook his head. "I'm not a healer, and the doctors and healers she went to couldn't do anything. She was in pain."

"So you fixed the pain. Was she in on the joke, or did you make the decision for her?"

"If the cops here weren't so stupid, they would have arrested Sebastian. We gave them all the clues."

A noise came from the back of the house—someone tripping over furniture maybe. Pablo turned his attention in that direction, then back to me. Fernandez screamed again, ragged and terrified.

I stepped toward Pablo and swung my wand like a club. It hit him in the head with a flash of light, and he went down, unconscious, before he hit the floor.

The cops rushed into the room, and I rushed to Fernandez. Tears ran down his face. He was blubbering and writhing in pain, but I noticed there was no movement in the lower part of his body.

"Get some null-magic cuffs on that guy!" I said, pointing at Pablo. There wasn't anything I could do for Sebastian. "Get those paramedics up here!" I looked at Barclay. "I sure hope there's a healer with them."

CHAPTER 40

The ambulance departed with Sebastian Fernandez, and a State Police car left with Pablo Arias. The doctor, who was a healer, walked over to where James and I watched the forensics team go in and out of the cabin. I wasn't sure if what they were doing was important, since we knew what had gone on in there.

"The bruising on his face is consistent with hitting the steering wheel of a car," the doctor told Barclay, "but it wasn't too bad. His nose is broken, but that's the worst of that damage. The real concern, and it's not something I can fix, either with medicine or magic, is his broken back."

"Was that from the car wreck?" James asked.

The doctor shook his head. "Magic. Torture, I would say. Each of the lowest four vertebrae are displaced, crushing the spinal cord. Almost impossible to say for sure, but I think it started where the spine joins with the pelvis, then the next vertebrae up, then the next. Incredibly painful."

"Pablo's mother died of a broken back from a fall," I said.

"Well, I don't think he's going to die—at least not right away. But with the general state of his health, his weight, and the emphysema, I wouldn't project his life expectancy as being very long."

"Emphysema?"

"Life-long smoker, is my guess."

"Any idea when I'll be able to interview him?" James asked.

"We need to stabilize him. Check with me the day after tomorrow. We'll probably call a specialist in from Pittsburgh."

James took me home. I was so tired I wanted to just fall in bed, but I was so cold that I took a hot bath first. It wasn't even Thanksgiving, and I wondered how I was going to survive the winter.

When I snuggled into the covers that night, I had difficulty falling asleep. Fernandez's screams haunted me.

James came by at lunch time, and I played the recording I had made with my phone.

"That certainly sounds like a confession," he said. "He killed his aunt trying to frame Sebastian Fernandez."

"With her cooperation," I said. "I have a feeling she was so doped up she probably didn't feel a thing."

"Unfortunately, I'll have to get him to repeat it—under caution, with a lawyer present. That's not going to be easy."

"Make him angry. He can't control his temper."

"True. The really difficult confession is going to be Fernandez's. I would still like to nail the CIA and Gary Akers. I certainly don't want someone like that as President."

"I wonder if Fernandez would trade immunity?"

"He might, but I don't have the authority to offer it. We'll see how it goes, and if I need to call in some help from the Council."

I called Kelly and invited her to dinner at my place with Barclay and me. He promised to drive her home, since she still wasn't driving. Her injury was also hampering her cooking, so she'd been eating most of her meals out. When I told her we had solved Alice's murder, she jumped at the chance.

A quick check of what I had in the pantry and fridge—sausage, cheese, tomatoes, onions, and bell peppers, along with some fettuccini—led to the decision to serve pasta and a salad.

She came by after work, and after making sure she wasn't taking any painkillers that would interact with alcohol, I opened a bottle of wine.

"The doctors gave me painkillers, but I've been using a potion Steven mixed up for me," she said. "It's much more effective, and it doesn't make me fuzzy."

I played the recording of Pablo, and she nodded. "Well, not the ending I expected, and I'm sure she hoped for a better end. This whole mess is going to sell books, though."

"Maybe more than you expect, if we can get Fernandez to flip on the CIA," James said.

"Do you really think he will?" she asked. "How is he doing?"

He took a deep breath. "We'll see. The doctors are saying I might get a chance to talk to him tomorrow. A specialist from Pittsburgh is here, and I think they're going to operate and insert a steel rod in his back. They don't expect that he'll ever walk again."

"And Maria?" Kelly asked.

James shook his head. "She's not doing well. Even with Ortiz and Lowell trying to calm her down, she doesn't seem to think Pablo did anything wrong."

"The line between justice and revenge is very thin sometimes," I said. "I wonder how a jury will treat him. I think almost everyone can sympathize with him, even if they don't agree with what he's done."

"What about Colby?" Kelly asked. "And Kathleen Furman?"

"Pablo's at the top of my list for both of them," James said.

"So Sebastian's only crime is pushing his wife off the balcony and stealing his stepchildren's inheritance thirty years ago?" I asked.

"Well, there's always the little matter of the death squads," James said. "We do have his confession to his wife's death recorded on Pablo's phone. We'd just have to edit out the screams and other sounds of torture."

I shuddered. "Ask him what caused him to run off the road."

"Okay. I'm a little curious about that myself."

"Do you still have Porter in jail?" Kelly asked.

"No, he's out on bail. Ballinger obtained an order from the judge that keeps him or any of his buddies—including their lawyer, Hawley—away from Fernandez. I have a couple of State detectives from Pittsburgh here keeping an eye on them."

"More cops in this town than crooks," Kelly said. "Why don't I feel safe?"

CHAPTER 41

James picked me up and took me with him to interview Sebastian Fernandez. A court stenographer, who carried a recording device, met us in the hospital lobby.

In the hallway outside his room at the hospital, we spoke with the doctors who were treating him—the healer who I had met at the cabin, and the specialist from the University of Pittsburgh.

"We have him sedated, both with drugs and with a magical potion. Any movement causes him incredible pain," the healer said.

"Either tomorrow or the next day," the specialist said, "we'll operate and insert a steel rod to stabilize his spine. The damage is just too much to heal."

"But we can talk to him?" James asked. "Is he lucid enough?"

"Oh, yes. But try and make it brief," the healer said.

We walked into the room with the stenographer, who set up her recorder and turned it on.

"Dr. Fernandez, I'm Lieutenant James Barclay of the Pennsylvania State Police. This is Dr. Savanna Robinson from Wicklow College who is here as a witness, and a stenographer appointed by the district court to record our conversation. Do you understand?"

"Yes. My body may be broken, but my mind is still functioning. How can I help you?"

Barclay took a seat in one of the chairs. "We have Pablo Arias in custody. I would like to hear your side of what happened. Do you wish to have a lawyer present?"

"Lawyer? Hell, no. Especially not that Hawley creature. He was never my lawyer. He's here to protect the CIA and their secrets. But what is anyone going to do to me now? They said they would protect me from Pablo, and instead they handed me over to him. Ask your questions, Lieutenant."

The story Fernandez told surprised us. He said Porter and Hawley sent him to Pittsburgh, where he would be flown to Spain and given a new identity. On his way out of town, he came around a corner and saw a deer standing in the road. He swerved to miss it, and crashed through the guardrail and into the river.

Two of Porter's men and Pablo Arias fished him out of the car and drove him to the cabin. The CIA goons left him with Pablo.

During Pablo's interrogation, Fernandez told him there was proof of his wife's will being fraudulently altered. There was also documentation of the drugs-for-guns scheme Chalmers and Akers ran to fund the Condor death squads. That was what Pablo was looking for at Fernandez's house when Barclay and I interrupted him.

"We didn't find anything like that," Barclay said.

"I'm not a fool," Fernandez responded. "It's in my office at the College. I just hoped he would go away and maybe you or someone else would catch him, or find me. I was grasping at straws, Lieutenant. He had already broken my back. Even killing me would have been better than what he did."

"Why did Porter want you dead?" I asked.

"Because Hawley told him to get rid of me. It's John Chalmers and Gary Akers. I know too much."

"Why did you kill Jefferson Colby?"

The ghost of a smile crossed his face. "I didn't. That was Pablo. He also tried to kill Kathleen Furman, but the woman is tougher than she appears."

"Are you willing to testify against Gary Akers?" James asked.

"Yes, and Peter Hawley, and Keith Porter as well. And if you give me a cigarette, I'll even testify against John Chalmers. The whole bloody bunch of them. But you'd probably better get a statement from me before I go into surgery. I may not come out, you know." He gave me a thin, knowing smile. "I may not be able to heal myself, but I know my condition probably better than my doctors do."

He went on to detail the death squads in Argentina and Uruguay, the scheme to buy weapons with cocaine money run by Chalmers and Akers, and the deal that the CIA made with Marcus LePage of the Witches' Council to move him out of South America to Wicklow. The documents in his office included names, dates, and even photographs. By the time we walked out of his hospital room, the stenographer's eyes were wide with shock, and I wondered if mine were, too.

James and I drove to the College, and I bypassed the locks on Fernandez's door, desk, and his files. We found the files on Operation Condor taped to the bottom of the drawers in his file cabinet. There was enough for a book all by itself—names, dates, places. Thorough and detailed documentation. Fernandez's documentation put what Alice had to shame.

CHAPTER 42

End of term. I had managed to survive a whole trimester at Wicklow. I was packed to leave on holiday and watched a video on my computer while waiting for my ride.

"Although I am deeply sorry, I won't be able to complete the work my constituents sent me here to do, my health issues will not allow me to continue serving in the United States Senate." The dignified-looking white-haired gentleman in an expensive suit said on the screen.

I snorted. Gary Akers's health issues were about to get a lot worse, as Kelly's book had gone to her editor the week before. The CIA had contacted him, and evidently had a frank discussion about what they would cover and what they would not. They had also attempted to have a discussion with her publisher, but between the publisher's lawyers and the Council's Arthur Balinger, that had gone nowhere.

John Chalmers's retirement from the CIA had been far less public, receiving a brief story that read almost like an obituary on page twelve of the Washington Post. I never did hear what happened to Keith Porter and his buddies, but I never bothered to enquire, either.

Sebastian Fernandez was living in a care facility in San Diego. A trust fund paid the bills. His doctors weren't optimistic about his life expectancy.

The majority of his money—more than twenty million dollars—went to Maria. I thought it was probably too little to make up for what he had taken from her, but at least she had the satisfaction of knowing she had been right about him all those years.

As for Pablo, Barclay flew with him to New Mexico, where a Council tribunal sentenced him to life in prison at the maximum-security facility in Antarctica. He showed no remorse for the murders. The Council psychologists diagnosed him as a pathological sociopath, and his magic made him too dangerous to ever turn him loose in society.

***

"So, are you ready for this?" I asked, standing in my living room with my bags.

James chuckled. "Probably not, but what the hell. I've always wanted to see Scotland."

He picked up one of my bags and held the door open for me. I picked up the other and walked out. His car sat at the bottom of the steps, trunk open and engine running.

"You know, you're only the second man brave enough to meet my mother, and it's been twenty years."

"As long as she lets me walk out instead of throwing my body over the wall, I'll be good."

I laughed and kissed him. "I'll protect you."

***

If you enjoyed ***The Revenge Game***, I hope you will take a few moments to leave a brief review on the site where you purchased your copy. It helps to share your experience with other readers. Potential readers depend on comments from people like you to help guide their purchasing decisions. Thank you for your time!

Get updates on new book releases, promotions, contests and giveaways! Sign up for my newsletter.

BOOKS BY BR KINGSOLVER
*ALSO AVAILABLE IN AUDIO FORMAT

Wicklow College of Arcane Arts
The Gambler Grimoire
The Revenge Game

The Rift Chronicles
Magitek**
War Song**
Soul Harvest**

The Crossroad Chronicles
Family Ties
Night Market
Ruby Road

Rosie O'Grady's Paranormal Bar and Grill
Shadow Hunter**
Night Stalker**
Dark Dancer**
Well of Magic**
Knights Magica**

The Dark Streets Series
Gods and Demons**
Dragon's Egg**

Witches' Brew**

The Chameleon Assassin Series

Chameleon Assassin**

Chameleon Uncovered**

Chameleon's Challenge**

Chameleon's Death Dance**

Diamonds and Blood**

The Telepathic Clans Saga

The Succubus Gift

Succubus Unleashed

Broken Dolls

Succubus Rising

Succubus Ascendant

Other books

I'll Sing for my Dinner

Trust